WRONG ALIEN:
A TERRAMATES NOVEL

LISA LACE

CONTENTS

CHAPTER 1

ANNALEE

I walked out of the childcare facility and stepped onto one of the transporter pads that had finally been installed around town, entering the coordinates closest to my second job. Some people refused to use the transporters. They were afraid their bodies might not emerge at their destination. Not me.

If there was a new device or gadget, I had it. If there was new technology somewhere, I was the first in line to try it. I swiped my phone over the payment processor and waited, tapping my fingers nervously against my thigh.

The moment stretched too long, and I bit my lip. Not again. A beep sounded, and the screen lit up: *Transaction incomplete due to insufficient funds.*

I couldn't believe it. I just got paid. How could my mother have spent it all already? I angrily pressed my lips together. Now I would have to dip into my college savings for everyday expenses, and that made me upset.

I had worked in different places since I was twelve years old. I had started out babysitting and working under the table at my father's restaurant. Then I got a job at a summer camp while I was in high school. When the restaurant closed, I got another job as a waitress at a fancy high-end restaurant where I made huge tips in addition to my paycheck.

When I finished high school, I started working at a childcare center, taking care of three and four-year-olds and running the preschool program — plus my job waiting tables at the new restaurant in the evenings. I was chronically exhausted and frankly, a little depressed at how little my life resembled my dreams.

I wanted to be a teacher. I had always wanted to, as long as I could remember. I wanted to walk into my classroom and see a bunch of sweet little shining faces looking up at me. I wanted to create fabulous lessons that would engage the kids and have them learning new things in such interesting ways that they wouldn't even know they were learning.

I wanted those sweethearts to come in and give me hugs and apples and pictures of people with arms coming out of their heads. And I wanted to be well-paid so I wouldn't have to work so hard anymore.

I also wanted a pony.

The screen was still flashing the insufficient funds message.

Right. Like I would ever get to become a teacher.

I tried not to get down on myself, but ever since my parents got divorced, my mother's life had taken a turn for the worse. She could hardly take care of herself anymore. She was always shopping for great 'deals', as she called them, and spending all the money. I needed to move out. Even if I had to pay all the rent myself, I could still save more if she wasn't spending everything I made. But I didn't see how she would manage without me.

What did I have to show from all my years of saving? I had saved nearly every penny, working summers and weekends, and almost every weeknight after school. Now that I had a full-time job, I tried to keep half my paycheck. My money disappeared like water down a drain.

I stepped off the transporter pad and began walking up the street. There was a cold drizzle coming down, and my uniform was getting damp. The restaurant was a thirty-minute walk away. Even though I took quick steps, I wasn't sure if I would make it on time.

How much did I have saved? Only one year's tuition. I didn't even want to go to the best university. All that work and I could only pay for one measly year. The thought made me want to cry.

I needed five hundred thousand credits to go to school and get an education degree. Tears sprang to my eyes as I walked. I wondered if I would ever be able to get that much money. I had been denied a student loan twice before because my mother couldn't pass the credit check. My father? I didn't know where he lived now or if he was even alive.

I sniffed and wiped at my eyes behind my Internet-connected glasses. When I blinked, the time popped up in front of my retinas. Shit. I was going to be late. I couldn't look like a mess when I got to work, so I made myself stop crying. It wouldn't help matters. The prettier

I looked, the better the tips. I fixed my make up as much as I could. I stood up straighter.

I would earn the money somehow. I would figure it out. I would become a teacher.

I had made this vow before to myself. Today with the clouds and the rain and the insufficient funds message, it was a bit much to take. Combined with being late for work...my manager hated when I was late...it all just seemed so hopeless. I sighed. The suffocating feeling of being trapped in a life I didn't want and had never asked for weighed me down.

If only there was some other way to get the money. But any other way was probably against the law. If I couldn't get a loan and it would take me years to save, the only other option for getting that much money was taking it.

I wouldn't do that. I snorted at the thought. I couldn't steal.

But if only there were a way to get the money that wasn't stealing...I felt my heart longing for some other way. An easier way than working my fingers to the bone for the next ten years. At this rate, I would be dead of exhaustion before I even had a chance to go to college.

If only there were some other way.

That night, as I sat on my bed at midnight, trying to relax enough to go to sleep, I pulled out my phone. Sometimes when I feel bad, I'll buy myself a new app. It's the only indulgence I allow myself because they're not very expensive. I know it sounds like something my mother would do: buying stuff when you're feeling down. But it was a small thing, and it made me happy.

I tapped on the store, and a page came up, showing different categories. I went through all my favorites but found nothing that interested me. Back on the front page, I noticed a new group. It was called *Love and Relationships*.

I hadn't had a boyfriend since high school. When would I find time to go on a date when I was working two jobs? In fact, I had turned down a guy who asked for a date tonight. Instead, I came home and hung out with myself. I preferred technology to people. Technology didn't let me down unless I forgot to update my phone.

But *Love and Relationships* seemed interesting.

I stared at the category, then tapped it to see what sort of apps were in there. The first one that I saw was one called M8r — as in mate-er. Cute. Developed by a company called TerraMates.

TerraMates? As in find your soul mate?

I tapped on it. What the hell could this app be for?

Oh my God. It was a mail-order bride service.

I giggled. Who would be desperate enough to use an app to arrange their marriage? I read through the description, laughing until I got to the fine print. You had to click twice to get there, but I always did. I never knew what things the app developers were trying to get away with, and I always read everything, especially the fine print.

At the bottom after reading all the other legalese, in what must have been 5 point font, it said they compensated female applicants for the worry and stress caused by leaving Earth and moving far away to an alien planet. At least, that's what I understood from the convoluted legal language.

I sat back in shock. So the men were *aliens*? And the women got paid to marry them? Holy shit.

Of course, my next question was *How much do they pay*?

"Do you wish to become a TerraMates bride, Miss Beauchene?" Mrs. Lynch, the owner of this TerraMates branch, looked over her glasses and down her long and pointy nose at me in an intimidating manner.

I worked with three-year-olds and senile, rich assholes who snap their fingers for my service. I wasn't intimidated easily.

"Actually," I said, ignoring her look and sitting forward in my seat. "I think there's been a bit of a misunderstanding. I wanted to find out more information. I found your app and was curious if your service might be a fit for what I'm looking for."

"Miss Beauchene, the only thing we provide are husbands. If you are looking for anything else, you need not apply," she said curtly.

How could anyone be that bitchy?

"Okay, then. Suppose I did want a husband, how does the process work?"

"You fill out an application and undergo various medical and psychological tests. Based on your application, and your test results, we may approve you. If you are approved, we match you with a male."

"An alien, you mean," I said. I needed everything spelled out.

"Miss Beauchene, please." I sat back to distance myself from the lightning bolts shooting from her eyes. "How are you not an alien to him? We do not tolerate bigotry here at TerraMates and will not approve anyone who displays such tendencies."

I raised both hands. "Hang on a minute. I'm not prejudiced, and as I recall, I didn't say anything derogatory about aliens. I'm trying to keep things straight in my mind. I want to make sure I understand what I'm getting into if I choose to apply to become a bride, Mrs. Lynch. Don't get your knickers in a knot."

"Miss Beauchene, we do not use such vulgar language here. You are already failing the interview portion of the evaluation."

"If I didn't apply yet, how can you start evaluating me?" I asked. My face was becoming hot. This wasn't fair.

"In my experience, Miss Beauchene, whether the woman knows it or not, by the time she arrives at our office, she has already made a decision about entering into an arranged marriage."

I stared at her, my swagger deflating.

"Those who are truly on the fence stay at home and remain on the fence. They don't come to our offices for more information."

I had the feeling if she knew what air quotes were, she would have put them around the words 'more information'.

I sat back and crossed my legs. If this was an interview, I had a few questions myself. "If I'm not passing, what am I doing wrong? What do the girls who pass do instead?"

She folded her hands together in her lap.

"You have an attitude problem, Miss Beauchene, and too much irreverence. You appear independent, which isn't necessarily a desirable quality. To be frank, you're not very pretty. Physical beauty is not a must-have, but it certainly helps."

I sat back in shock. No one had ever told me I was unattractive to my face. I thought about my appearance. I was wearing glasses, and my hair was in a messy braid behind my head. Wild strands of hair were escaping and rioting around my face. I hadn't put on any make-up, and I probably had bags under my eyes from last night.

It was my day off. I was going to pick up some groceries for dinner when I happened to pass by the TerraMates office and thought I would pop in and get a brochure. I wasn't looking particularly glamorous today, but I had always thought I was mildly pretty in a girl-next-door sort of way. Not beautiful by any stretch of the imagination, but easy on the eyes.

What did this woman know anyway?

The receptionist didn't give me a pamphlet. She led me into Mrs. Lynch's office and asked me to wait. Apparently the interview started as soon as Mrs. Lynch walked through the door.

"I'm not saying you shouldn't apply. We have assisted many potential brides similar to you who have been satisfied with their alien husband."

"Happy?" I repeated distantly. I wasn't listening to her. I couldn't get over the fact that I wasn't pretty enough to be a mail-order bride. Surely, an alien who used such a service couldn't afford to be choosy. If they wanted to be picky, they could go and find a three-eyed wife of their own.

"Yes, we have a high rate of..."

"Divorce?" I finished for her. I was confident that was what she was going to say.

"No," she said, giving me a steely glance. "We have a very low divorce rate, which you would know if you did any research on our company. Very few of our women request a divorce when they complete the required year."

"I don't believe it," I said, folding my arms over my chest.

"You don't have to believe something for it to be true," she said, opening a drawer in her desk and taking out a tablet. "What I was going to say was that we have a very high rate of satisfaction among our women. Please fill this in."

"How do you know I want to apply?" I said. "Especially after what you said about me?"

She looked at me for a moment. A tiny smile appeared on her withered face and she looked amused. I wondered what her story was. How had she become such an unpleasant person? The smile disappeared quickly, but I wouldn't forget it.

I didn't think a person like Mrs. Lynch knew how to smile.

"How do I know you want to apply?" She studied me closely. "Because you didn't walk out when I said you were ugly, my dear."

She pushed the tablet across the desk towards me and stood up.

"After you complete the forms, come down the hall. We have a nurse on staff that will perform your medical examination. There's one more thing."

"Yes?" I said blankly.

"You didn't ask, but your compensation is five hundred thousand credits. I suggest you don't do it for the money. That sort of thing never works out."

I stared at the door long after it had closed. Eventually, I gazed at the tablet. I reached out and turned it on, watching my hands move by themselves.

Everything about TerraMates was crazy. But 500,000 credits would pay for everything. Still, being a mail-order bride felt like prostitution no matter what the contract said. I knew I should get up and walk out the door right now. I wasn't really going to do this, was I?

But a tiny part of me knew that I was. I was sick of this life. I was sick of never getting anywhere. And I was sick to death of wishing and hoping for my dreams to come true and never seeing them happen.

I wasn't going to wish and hope any longer. I was going to make my dream of becoming a teacher a reality. And it was only going to take a year.

No doubt it would be an eventful year, but maybe that was a good thing. I had never left my hometown. I worked six days a week. I was tired. And I felt old, like I had never lived.

This was going to be an adventure and the beginning of a different life.

That's when I knew I had already made the decision. Butterflies fluttered in my stomach at the thought.

I was getting married.

CHAPTER 2

JESSE

"Father, I have no desire to get married." The fire on the hearth crackled in the background of our conversation.

"Then you have no desire to take over the farm."

"There must be another way to satisfy the requirements."

"There is no way but marriage. The law explicitly states you must have a wife to inherit while I am alive, and with good reason. You cannot expect to raise and train a herd of hundinlark without assistance."

"The help could be anyone. I could hire a worker."

"You know hundinlark require a very sensitive touch, and they respond better to women. You can't have a bunch of men caring for your herd. I'm sorry, son, but they'll be better if a woman raises them."

"Why can't I hire women to work for me?"

"You know they won't do that, and none would work for you even if they would work for someone else."

"You're being ridiculous."

"That's not what years of tradition say."

"I don't mean it's ridiculous that hundinlark respond better to women. I mean the rest of it."

I stood up and paced while my father sat calmly in his chair by the fire. The house had been part of our family for generations — since The Before Times.

"It doesn't matter what you want. You cannot inherit the farm unless you have a wife. Period. End of story, son. Why are you suddenly upset now? It has always been this way."

"Not always, Father. There was a time when we had choices," I said. I knew I was heading into dangerous waters, but I couldn't stop myself.

My father raised his eyebrows. "You don't want to return to our lifestyle before The End, do you?" he asked. "That way led to our civilization's destruction. Millions of people died. All of our cultures were nearly snuffed out in an instant. And it was due to freedom and..."

He wouldn't say the word technology but I knew that's what he meant. I wasn't afraid of a word.

"It was not the technology that pushed the button, Father," I pointed out. I stopped on the hearth so the side of my body that faced the fire was burning hot and the side that faced the room was cold. "It was just a person."

"But it did create a situation where one person could destroy everything with a button, Jesse."

"I know, Father. I don't want to go back in time. But I do wish we could abolish some of our oldest customs that no longer make sense. One of these is the requirement of marriage to inherit the land."

"Well, it's not you or me that will do away with them. That's for the king and the council to figure out. Perhaps it will be the queen who will decide, if King Murtaugh is as ill as they say. Marsaline will make a good queen if he ever gets out of the way. We are fortunate she is only a second cousin, and not closely related to him. We will have a very different reign if she ever takes the throne. You will, at least," he added, dropping his eyes.

"Do not speak that way, Father. I will find the best healers to tend to you. You will live to see your grandchildren."

He smiled sadly. "Would that I could, Jesse. It will be enough if I see you take over the farm before I die. Do you not desire a wife? Many lovely girls live in the village. There must be someone there who has caught your eye."

I had plenty of desire for the young women of the village; unfortunately, they had no desire for me. The odd one would lie with me. Perhaps she thought I was handsome, in spite of my past, or maybe a friend dared her to.

None would consider marrying me. A man with my reputation would not make a good husband.

"It is not a case of desire, Father, and you know it."

"Jesse, your transgression was long ago. It was the mistake of a boy."

"They haven't forgotten, and none of them would consider my proposal. I don't intend to humiliate myself by asking," I said, drawing myself up straight.

My father frowned. "Perhaps you are correct about changing the old customs," he said. "It's not right for them to continually punish a good man because of something that happened in the past. Have you considered marrying outside our village?"

We looked at each other. We both knew that if no one in my village would have me, the chances of a stranger taking the risk were slim to none. Even if such a woman existed, she was not the kind of woman I wanted as a wife. I sat down on a wooden bench and put my head in my hands.

"It is impossible, Father."

"Jesse, I cannot continue to run the farm," he said, his eyes hungry with desperation. He coughed hard while I stood by helpless to assist him. "I am too ill."

"I know, Father. I know."

"And if I die without you inheriting our land, someone else can acquire it."

"I'll think of something. I won't let strangers have our farm."

He sat back after the coughing fit. He looked different these days; he seemed old and tired.

"See that you do, Jesse. There is nothing more important to me than keeping the farm in the family."

"I will."

He nodded. His eyes started to close, and I left him. It was time for him to nap after dinner.

My father could not bear to think of our family's hard-earned hundinlark farm being turned over to the hands of strangers who would never love it the way the Melnyks always had.

I would find a woman. It couldn't be that hard.

After the fourth fruitless week of traveling to all the villages in the nearby area, I was beginning to wonder if I had been overly optimistic. I knew I was going to need help — and not the legal kind.

I walked into the inn and looked around. The innkeeper was standing at the bar, polishing glasses. The place was still empty because it was early afternoon.

"Can I help you?"

"Perhaps," I said. "I'm looking for a man called Porter."

"Porter? What's his family name?"

"That's his name. He goes by Porter."

"Oh, that one. He usually comes in around dinnertime. If you want to speak to him, you'll need to return later." He eyed me suspiciously. "Why do you want to see him?"

"I'm an old friend visiting the area, and I wanted to have a pint with him."

The innkeeper didn't believe a word I said. "Whatever you say, stranger."

"I'll see you again."

The man nodded and watched me all the way out the door. I could feel his gaze boring into my back as I went outside.

Porter was my oldest friend. I had known him since we were ten. We had been through some tough times together. One day, he disappeared, and I never knew where he went.

The rumor was he was on the run from the Bureau, but I never got confirmation. I had never tried to find him.

That was before. Now I needed him, and I had tracked him here. I was sure he was the only person on Yordbrook who could help me with my problem.

A few hours later, I was at the inn again with a pint of ale in front of me. When Porter entered, he was laughing with a bunch of men who were listening to a story he told. Only Porter could simultaneously be hiding out and remain the center of attention. He glanced around the room and looked at everyone briefly. He didn't react, but I knew he had seen me.

I finished my drink and got up to leave. I knew he would follow when he had the opportunity. I waited in the clearing nearby where I heard he conducted his transactions, my cloak wrapped close around me and my hood drawn up to protect against the drizzling rain.

After a while, the area around me was becoming dark and the rain had stopped. I thought about going back to the inn and finding my bed. Perhaps he couldn't come tonight. As I was about to give up and leave, I heard footsteps approaching me, and a woman softly giggling.

When the couple entered the clearing, I recognized Porter immediately, but not the girl on his arm.

"Melnyk. How are you? It's been too long," he said, coming forward. We embraced and he clapped me roughly on the back.

"Why did you bring a woman?" I whispered before he stepped away.

"Last time you wanted a woman to lie with you and not look at you like you were a Renegade. I assumed you wanted it again. She's already had enough morelia. She doesn't care who you are as long as you have a cock to fuck her."

His response was unexpected. "I wanted a woman, not a whore," I said.

"She's not a whore," he said. He sounded offended. "She's the miller's daughter. She's had a few drinks, and you know how horny morelia makes the women. They get uncomfortable if someone doesn't fuck them. You better take her voluntarily before she makes you."

I looked at his companion. She was sexy, and it had been a long time. She smiled at me in a way that made me instantly hard.

I thought about lifting her skirt. I could bury myself inside her and have her hot wetness clench around me when she came. Morelia ensured loud, ecstatic orgasms. There wasn't much for the man to do. Just put it in and fuck. It didn't take long, either.

Porter was a good friend.

"Okay, but wait at the inn. I need to speak with you."

"Excellent," he said, pounding me on the back again. "It shouldn't take long. Look at her. She's already panting."

She was. Her hands were on her breasts, and she was playing with herself. I couldn't resist going to her as Porter left. She didn't say a word, only pulled me in for a kiss that was hot, wet, and included a lot of tongue.

I pulled on her dress, and her breasts spilled out. I had to taste them. I bent to take one in my mouth. She moaned. She was a live wire.

After only a few minutes, she was begging me to fuck her and desperate to have me inside her. I pushed her up against a tree and raised her skirt. She stuck out her bare ass toward me, trembling with desire. I touched her. She was dripping wet and slippery. It had been a long time for me.

I slid into her slowly to allow her body to accommodate me. She was a small woman, and I was a fairly big man. She moaned and writhed under me as I penetrated her, but soon I was in as far as I could penetrate.

Then I did what any man in my position would do. I fucked her until she came. When we finished, I walked her back to the inn, put her to bed in one of the rooms to sleep, and left a bag of coins on the bedside table.

After I had cleaned up, I went to find Porter. I needed to thank him for the woman and ask him to help get me a wife.

"Well?" he said when I joined him at his table. He grinned at me and waggled his eyebrows. "She's good, huh?"

"Amazing," I said. "Was the morelia her idea or yours?"

"Hers, of course. She was hoping to get me to fuck her, but the idea of a new guy interested her more."

Now it was my turn to raise my eyebrows.

"She likes her sex, and she's too young to get married. She appreciates it when I come to town for a roll in the hay...or the grass...or the bed. She doesn't care where, as long as she comes. She likes morelia because it guarantees an orgasm for her."

"She's not old enough to wed, Porter? That's playing with fire. And I don't particularly want to get burned."

"You mean you don't want to get burned *again*."

"Maybe," I said. "Next time bring me one who's of age."

"There's gratitude for you," he said, rolling his eyes. "I'll do the best I can, but I'm not running a store here."

"It must be nice to have a girl in every village who's willing to spread her legs for you," I said, unable to keep the resentment out of my voice.

He shrugged. "There's always women who want to come to and in my bed," he said.

I shook my head. "Not so much for a Renegade."

"I'm not the one who found a piece of technology and hid it," he said, laughing at me. "You were fifteen. That's old enough to know better, Jesse." He shook his finger at me, like an elder.

"I suppose I was, and I've got to live with the consequences. I don't like it when my decisions hurt other people. My father's sick."

"Is he getting worse?" All the teasing had gone out of him, and I saw only worry on Porter's face for the man

25

who was like a father to him. "But you haven't inherited yet. If he dies..."

"It goes up for sale, and we both know who'll buy it."

"Sanderman." The richest man in our valley was always buying farms from people in trouble.

I nodded.

"Strangers in our house, Porter. They'll let the field rot and the hundinlark go wild."

"Or make more money off of it than your family ever did," he said.

"Either way, it will be a disaster. I can't let that happen," I told him, leaning forward.

"So don't." He looked around the room. "You only have to find a wife."

"That's the problem," I said.

That got his attention. He turned his shrewd eyes on me. "Why is that a problem?"

"It's the same reason I came to you last time. If girls don't want to sleep with a Renegade, imagine trying to find one willing to marry a Renegade."

"Show me the tattoo."

I rolled my eyes but pulled up my sleeve. He had seen it many times before, but I knew he wouldn't stop asking until I showed him again. They had done it without anesthetic, of course. Renegades don't get a drink for the pain.

The tattoo was the letter **R**. Renegades were people who accepted and wanted technology to come back. There was an underground movement trying to bring science back to our planet. I shivered at the thought. Being caught as a member of the Underground would be worse than being tattooed and shunned.

The **R** made me an outsider in a society that had decreed technology evil. Anyone who didn't share their views was evil, too. Most people would rather die than touch a piece of technology.

Since birth, the fact that high technology had almost destroyed us was drilled into our brains. Our ancestors had decided to ban it rather than risk annihilating our entire civilization again. I wasn't sure that technology had been the problem, but I knew better than to voice such views in public.

Now all I wanted to do was please my father, inherit the farm, and marry a girl. I wanted to be normal and live quietly, with no memory of my mistake following me through life.

Was that too much to ask?

As I saw the disapproving glances of the people around me who had seen my tattoo, I realized it might be, and I quaffed the ale Porter ordered for me.

He grinned. "It's a work of art."

"You only think that way because you don't have one," I said bitterly. We had discovered the device together. He was smart enough to leave it where it was. Although he had touched it, he had gloves on and didn't move it.

I had been unable to resist the shiny object. I needed to pick it up and take it home with me. I thought I had concealed it safely under the brick floor.

What a fool.

"We each make our choices."

"How about you choose to help me now, Porter? You owe me."

"I'm not sure if I owe you, Melnyk, but I'll help you for old time's sake."

I didn't care why he helped me as long as he did.

"What do you need?" he asked, leaning forward.

"I need a wife. As soon as possible."

"How do you expect me to help you get one of those?"

"Porter. I know you have ways. And access to things I don't."

He pulled at the collar of his shirt and shifted in his seat.

"What are you asking?"

"No one on the planet will marry me willingly," I said. "Not with this."

I patted my shoulder. I had hidden the tattoo under my shirt again.

"Let me get this straight. You're hoping an ignorant off-worlder will marry you?"

I didn't say anything. We both knew he could assist me if he wanted.

"It will cost something. You know access to such things is expensive," he said.

"How much?"

"A quarter of your herd."

"Never," I said. "Father would never agree to that."

"Not even to keep the family farm?" Porter asked innocently.

He was right. My father might agree if I told him what it was for, as long as he didn't know what Porter was going to do.

"You know I'm not gouging you, Jesse," he said. "Access is very expensive, especially these days with the Bureau of Purity on our backs."

I pressed my lips together. I knew I was making a deal with the devil, but there was no one else I could ask.

"Okay," I said, and Porter could barely contain his excitement. His hands balled into fists, and he had a big smile on his face. A quarter of a herd of fully-trained hundinlark was quite the prize.

"She must be willing," I said, starting to tick off each requirement on my fingers. "She must be of age, not have an aversion to technology..."

Whoops. I stopped myself and looked around to see if anyone had heard my mistake. Porter gave me an incredulous look.

"Willing," I repeated. "Of age. And other things." I thought for a moment. "It would be nice if she were pretty."

"Jesse, beggars can't be choosers."

"Fine. I don't care about her appearance, but the other items are non-negotiable. Don't forget."

"I won't," he said. His demeanor was serious now that we were talking business.

"A willing wife, who is of age and likes...things."

"That's right," I said.

Porter stood up.

"Have the hundinlark shipped to me when I send word that I've found her. If I can find someone, I will bring her within the month." He offered me his hand, and we shook. He started moving towards the door, but then stopped and turned back. I glanced up at him, wondering if he had forgotten something.

"For the record, Jesse," he said, his face solemn. "I'm sorry about the **R**."

I looked down at the floor. "It's not your fault."

"Of course it's not," he said. "But I'm still sorry."

I looked up, but he had left already. All I had to do now was to sit on my hands and wait. And convince my father to give away a quarter of our herd.

I wondered if she would be pretty, and whether I could live with an ugly wife if she weren't.

I tried to remember that the only thing that mattered was saving the farm. All women look the same in a dark bedroom, right? Isn't that what Porter always said?

I sighed. It was going to be a long month.

CHAPTER 3

ANNALEE

"What do you mean I can't take my phone?" I asked, feeling panicked. My phone had all my music, my movies, my books, my contacts, my messages, and my photos. It was how I paid for things. It was how I entertained myself. It had my memories. My whole life was on that device. I wasn't handing it over to a grim-faced woman who had never had a day of fun in her life.

More than anything else, there was a picture of Kyle on my phone. I wasn't leaving that image behind. I had promised him I would always keep it with me while I was gone.

Kyle wasn't my boyfriend. He was a four-year-old in my preschool class. I smiled as I remembered the way he looked. Kyle was a little boy whose overworked single mother hardly had time for him. She did the best she could with the time she had and always asked how he was doing. She wanted him to excel in school so he could make a better life for himself. He was a brilliant child and was already learning how to read.

When I told my classes that I wouldn't be coming back for a long time, he was heartbroken and sobbed uncontrollably until his mother came to pick him up. Then he didn't want to say good-bye to me.

We took a selfie together. I promised him I would keep the picture with me everywhere I went in the galaxy so he would be with me. The promise comforted him. And my heart, which felt like it was breaking at the thought of leaving all the students in my preschool classes, felt a little better.

"There is no technology allowed on Yordbrook, Miss," the customs officer repeated, bringing me back to the present.

"Surely there must be some exceptions," I said.

The woman shook her head. "How can you come to a planet like Yordbrook without knowing anything about the planet?" she asked, rolling her eyes. "You're certainly in for some culture shock."

TerraMates had sent me some folders about Jesse and his planet. I had no time to read them because I had been working overtime to buy new clothes. I intended to bring the information to read on the space flight, but my mother had tried to help by cleaning up for me. The folders had been missing ever since.

My mother. I felt like grinding my teeth at the thought of her. I had returned from TerraMates that day to find her with a new boyfriend. A couple of days later, she asked me to move out. The timing was great because I didn't have to worry about what she would do without me.

But it still hurt that she cast aside her daughter as soon as she met Marlo. Had she been using me the whole time for my money? Now that she had a new supplier, did she no longer need me?

Right now, I had even bigger problems than my mother.

"What happens to my devices if I leave them here?" I asked.

"There's no if, sweetie. Technology is not allowed on Yordbrook. If you want to beam down, you have to leave everything behind."

"Okay...where does my stuff go?"

"It's all stored until you return," she said.

"Can I have a minute?" I asked, and she smiled, shaking her head again.

"Sure, dear," she said. The agent waved the next person in line forward. "You can have a minute to say goodbye to your belongings."

"You're hilarious," I said, giving her an annoyed look.

"Don't forget, I'll search you when you come back," she called after me.

I pulled my luggage with me to the bathroom and locked the door, sitting down on the toilet. I could not leave it all here.

I wondered what I could do. I would let go of the big items like the computer and tablet, and the less important things like my glasses that accessed the Internet and my music-playing ring. I would wear my regular glasses. The frames were way uglier than the Internet-capable glasses, but they would have to do.

But my phone had to come with me. It couldn't be that big of a deal. It could recharge the battery from any light source. But how would I smuggle it?

I looked at it thoughtfully. It was a piece of two-by-two inch adjustiplast stuck to the back of my hand. Adjustiplast was state-of-the-art plastic and could become hard or soft as necessary. It adhered to one's skin, so the wearer didn't have to carry it. I couldn't hide it somewhere on my person because the customs agent would find it in the search.

That left body orifices. Gross. I wrinkled my nose. Swallow it or put it inside me?

I didn't like either choice. My stomach acid wouldn't hurt it; adjustiplast was impervious to most things. A little hydrochloric acid wasn't going to destroy it. But how would I get it back out? Either vomiting or waiting to pass it in the toilet didn't appeal to me. Even swallowing it might be harder than I thought.

The other option was to put it inside me, like a tampon. That certainly seemed like the best choice, although it was still distasteful. When I thought about the alternative, I knew I had to do it.

I remembered Kyle's tearful eyes and the promise. I wasn't one of those people who lie to kids to get them to shut up. If I told him I would keep it with me, I would keep my word, just as if I had made the promise to an adult. In fact, it was more important to me that I keep my word to Kyle.

A promise made to a child is sacred.

I peeled off the phone and washed it carefully. I pulled down my pants and underwear. I stared at myself in the mirror and wondered if I was doing the right thing.

Without thinking too much, I took a deep breath and rolled the phone up, then concealed it. I hoped the agent wasn't going to do a full body cavity examination.

The die was cast. My phone was coming with me, and I was keeping my promise to Kyle.

It occurred to me that I was starting my year on Yordbrook by breaking one of their most important laws. But I quickly realized that when I had beamed up from Earth, I needed to leave behind my old ideas about what was right and what wasn't.

I had always followed the rules my whole life and where had it got me? Nowhere. I was going to follow my heart from now on. Maybe it would lead me to something better.

I washed my hands and stepped out of the bathroom, ready to beam down to my new home.

They didn't bring out a big welcoming party on Yordbrook. "Here," a sour-faced woman said roughly as she handed me a large pile of clothes.

"What's this?" I said.

"You won't need the things you brought or what you're wearing," she said, glancing distastefully at the clothes in my luggage.

"Do I have to leave them here like my devices?"

The woman cut me off with a sharp movement of her hand slicing through the air. "We do not speak of such things. You will not have to leave your clothes here, but it is inappropriate to wear such garments." She glanced in disgust at the cute pair of jeans I wore. I had worked extra shifts to buy them. I wanted to have fresh things when I arrived at my new home.

I stopped when I realized her implications. "Are you telling me I can't wear pants here?" I asked.

"Only men wear trousers," she said. She sounded like my question was ridiculous.

"Maybe on this planet," I said. "On Earth, it's a common practice."

"You are no longer on Earth," she reminded me with a stern look.

I didn't think I needed reminding. If I were back home, I certainly wouldn't be hiding my phone. I shifted slightly.

"Well?" she said, looking back at me. "Take your approved outfit in the changing room and get dressed."

I hesitated only a moment and followed orders. To my embarrassment, I did have to call her in one time to explain how to do up one of the pieces of under-clothing. The rest was self-explanatory. When taken together, everything looked like a costume from seventeenth-century Earth, my favorite period of ancient history.

There was a shift, which looked like a slip you would wear under a fancy dress. I left the corset as loose as I dared. I wasn't going to be squeezing my organs and making myself sick. Still, I tied it tightly enough to keep my breasts from bouncing around. The outfit didn't come with a bra. There was an underskirt, an overskirt, and a dress that went over the whole package and laced up in the front.

I didn't know the names of all the parts; I just remembered a few things from history class and historical fiction books.

It all felt very complicated. I was already intimidated, but I had to suck it up. When I went back out, the woman burst out laughing and helped me adjust something I had put on backward. I pressed my lips together as she fixed it, and said thank-you when she finished.

"There," she said. "I suppose you'll do." She didn't seem sure I would do at all. "Your ride is here," she said.

"I'm all done with customs, then?" I asked. The process had been arduous. There had been a search and verification of my documents at the space station. Once I beamed down, I was searched again (in case I smuggled something in transit, I suppose) and more documents needed signing. I think they said I wouldn't ruin their world with technology, or something of that nature. I hadn't read them in great detail, but I signed them so I could move on. After changing my clothes, it looked like I was finally finished, and my fiance was here.

"You're done here," she said. "Good luck."

"Thank you," I said, smiling at her.

"He's out front," she said. I nodded, pushing open the door.

When I walked out of the building, I was astonished at the beauty around me. It appeared to be the height of summer here. The grass was green, the trees were in full leaf, and there were flowers everywhere. I looked up and saw one sun approaching the horizon, one overhead, and one rising on the opposite side of the planet.

Three suns? That seemed like overkill.

"You must be Annalee," a deep voice said, and I turned my head.

"And you must be the man I'm going to marry?" I said.

He shook his head. "No such luck, my dear," he said. "The name's Porter. I'll be taking you to your fiance."

In contrast to the customs agent, Porter seemed gracious and kind. He carried my luggage for me and helped me into the carriage. Even so, I had a nagging feeling at the back of my mind that he was laughing at me behind his serious face.

There was a team of small creatures that looked like goats attached to the carriage, like reindeer to Santa's sleigh. But there were no reins. Porter gave commands, and they obeyed him. They were a native species to this planet that could be domesticated and used their horns like hands. Weird but cute. I was impressed.

It took us a few weeks to get to my future husband's farm. Porter was a gentleman the whole time. When we needed to sleep, he got us separate rooms at inns on the way.

I quickly got used to using composting toilets in little huts behind the main houses. I had to scoop some sawdust or grass clippings to cover things up once I did my business. But the places were nothing like the outhouses I was familiar with on Earth. They smelled sweet and fresh, like sawdust or grass clippings. They were kept scrupulously clean and insect-free.

One thing I wouldn't get used to was the lack of electricity. They only used candles for lights and still did many things by hand. But the food was incredible, and the weak artificial light meant I could see the stars at night.

No electricity meant no gadgets. I continually glanced at the back of my hand, unconsciously looking for my phone. Whenever I wanted to learn something new about this planet I wanted to look it up on the Internet, and I couldn't. Even though I had traveled through space to get here, I felt like I was living in the stone age.

All in all, this planet wasn't bad, but I missed modern living. I was also getting nervous about meeting my fiance. Each day that passed only made me more anxious. I tried asking Porter about him, but he hadn't said anything interesting. As we drove the last few miles to the village, I tried again.

"Porter," I said. "Tell me about Jesse."

"There's not much to tell, Annalee. I've known him a long time. He's a good man. And you shouldn't believe what people will say about him."

"What's that supposed to mean?" I said.

"You're an off-worlder, so you don't know what it's like here. People are particular about things. They think that there's only one way to live. Jesse feels differently, but that doesn't mean that he's bad or wrong."

I didn't say anything. It seemed like he was avoiding talking about something. It was the first time Porter had spoken with me honestly and not through a polished veneer.

He pulled into the yard, and a young man came out and started unharnessing the cute alien goats. I looked at Porter, but he shook his head. Apparently this wasn't Jesse.

Porter came around and offered me his hand. I took it and climbed down. At first I had tried to preserve my independence and modern woman status, but it didn't take me long to realize that there was a reason women needed so much help in the past. It had to do with the restrictions clothing put on them.

That's why being able to wear pants was such a big symbol for the feminists of the late twentieth century. It represented freedom from needing men to help us because of our stupid outfits.

Here I was, many years after those women had fought for our right to wear whatever we wanted. I was back to needing a man to help me in and out of vehicles. I silently asked my foremothers for forgiveness as he helped me leave the carriage.

In frustration, I straightened the skirts that made me dependent on a man just to climb out of a vehicle, shaking them out and trying to get rid of the dust which had settled on my clothing. The task seemed impossible, so I settled for brushing them off the best I could. They still looked dirty. I checked my bust — cleavage, yes, plenty of that with the corset and low-cut dress.

The wife of the most recent innkeeper helped make my long brown hair. A bun was one of the acceptable hair styles on this planet. By this time, the bun had eroded, and my hair was slipping out all over the place. It never seemed to stay where I put it.

I wore a royal blue cloak with the hood up. It covered my hair and helped conceal my untamed mane. I pushed my glasses back up my nose and supposed this was as good as I was going to look after three weeks of travel. I needed a shower, and I wasn't sure when the next one was coming.

When a man walked into the yard from the fields behind the inn, I immediately knew he was Jesse. It wasn't just because I recognized him from his pictures from the TerraMates office back on Earth. I felt myself come alive as soon as our eyes met. He had an aura of power about him. And charisma. And he had bad-boy stamped on his forehead.

Unfortunately, he didn't feel the same way about me. He took one look at me and frowned.

"Is this the one?" he asked Porter. He didn't even look at me and talked right over my head.

"That's her," Porter said. "Annalee Beauchene, meet your fiance, Jesse Melnyk."

Jesse moved toward me. "It's good to meet you, Miss Beauchene," he said. It didn't sound like he meant it at all. "Would you like to come inside and wash up or rest?

Perhaps you can get something to eat before we go back to my father's farm and meet him?"

Meet his father? I hadn't thought that I would have to meet his family. But I supposed it might be possible if we were going to get married. Thank goodness he wouldn't have to meet my parents...not that I really had a family anymore.

"Nice to meet you, too," I said, trying a curtsy. He didn't smile, and Porter was clearly trying not to laugh.

"Yes, I'd like to wash up, please. And have a meal," I said, feeling bleak for the first time since my adventure started. I stared at the back of my hand, wishing for the comfort of my phone to distract me from my unhappiness.

My future husband didn't seem to like me, and he wasn't as much of a gentleman as Porter had been. He made me open the door for myself. Not that I couldn't, I reminded myself. I was a modern woman. Still, it had been nice to feel special when Porter opened doors for me. I guess I had gotten used to it.

"Porter, will you join us?" he asked.

Porter looked back and forth between us, grinning. "Of course, Jesse," he said. "I'd pay to see this show."

CHAPTER 4

JESSE

While I waited for Porter and my fiancee, I had been checking out the innkeeper's fields. Although he was an idiot in some respects, Myron Dublay was becoming a decent farmer. I stopped when I got to the edge of the yard, surveying all the people. Porter had sent word they would arrive in the afternoon, but I didn't know when.

At that moment, I spotted him helping a woman out of a carriage. She was here.

I watched as she descended gracefully from the vehicle. Her form was pleasing. Full breasts, a narrow waist, and wide hips. She would bear children well.

I supposed I should stop hiding at the edge of the yard and meet her. I felt nervous, which made me irritated. There was no reason to be nervous.

And yet I was. I gathered myself and walked toward her. I had met more intimidating people than her, so there was no reason I should be anxious.

She turned her head and watched my approach. Her eyes widened in...appreciation? I filed that information away in the back of my mind. I ignored the shot of energy that went through me when our eyes met. This woman was a means to an end. I had no desire to become emotionally entangled with her.

45

As I got closer to her body, I noticed she was somewhat plain and unkempt. Her hair was a mess, her skirts full of dust, and she wore large spectacles on her face.

Apparently I wasn't getting a lovely woman to look at over the breakfast table.

"Is this the one?" I said to Porter, avoiding direct eye contact. I didn't want to have to look at her more than was necessary. I clung tightly to the thought that all women look beautiful in a dark bedroom.

"That's her," he said. "Annalee Beauchene, meet your fiance, Jesse Melnyk."

He spoke respectfully to Annalee, but when he turned to me, he smirked and winked.

I rolled my eyes. Where had he found this wench? I checked out her cleavage — ample. I supposed she would do.

"It's good to meet you, Miss Beauchene," I said, formally. "Would you like to come inside and wash up or rest? Perhaps you can get something to eat before we go back to my father's farm and meet him?"

She looked like she hadn't been expecting me to ask her anything, but she recovered quickly.

"Nice to meet you, too," she said, doing a clumsy curtsy that reminded me she only looked like a Yordbrook woman. She had likely never curtsied before because she was from another planet — a modern world, with modern things. I frowned. It might be harder than I thought to hide that she wasn't from around these parts. The notion hadn't occurred to me when I asked for Porter's help.

"Yes, I'd like to wash up, please. And have a meal," she said, the light going out of her eyes when she looked at me. It was as if all the spunk had drained out of her. I wondered what had caused the change. She hadn't looked like that when she arrived.

"Porter, will you join us?" I clapped him on the shoulder and squeezed it tightly.

"Of course, Jesse." His eyes twinkled with amusement. "I'd pay to see this show."

The bastard. He would pay for setting me up with this homely lass. She had better be amazing in bed.

Despite my dreams, after she cleaned up the woman didn't look much better than before she went inside. I wondered if she had a brush. I tried to remember I was doing this for my father so he could die in peace. She was something necessary, and I would have to adjust.

The three of us sat down at a table. The innkeeper's wife, Isabella, brought us fresh baked bread and butter, along with three plates and a knife. She smiled at me.

We had a morelia encounter when we were both teenagers, and apparently she had never forgotten it. At least, that was how it seemed to me the two times she tried to get me to have an affair with her. I had turned her down, but she was difficult to resist.

I didn't blame her, of course. Myron couldn't be much fun in bed. I had certain standards and sleeping with married women isn't something I did.

Porter offered the girl the bread and butter first. The look on her face when she tasted it gave me hope. I glanced at Porter, and he waggled his eyebrows at me. She didn't notice because she was busy enjoying the bread.

Her eyes were closed. She let out a gentle moan when she took the first bite. "This is incredible."

"You've not tasted bread before?" I said. "It's a based on a plant we call 'wheat' on this world." She was from another planet, I supposed.

"Of course I've had bread," she said, a sparkle returning to her eyes. "But this is the best I've ever tasted."

Porter laughed then. "That's what she says at every inn," he explained. He liked this girl.

"Not every one," she said, objecting. "The one with the pig on the sign didn't have good bread." She turned to me. "It really didn't. It's a good thing we only stopped there for a snack and some rest. I couldn't have stayed there overnight."

Porter buttered another piece and handed it to her. "Thank you," she said, giving him a gracious smile.

I frowned at him. Was he flirting with my soon-to-be-wife? He lifted his hands to me, palms up, and she looked back and forth between us.

"So, you two are friends?" she said, addressing the question to Porter.

"Aye," he said, grinning stupidly at me. I rolled my eyes.

"For how long?" she asked, taking another bite of bread and chewing.

"A long time," Porter said. "Since we were boys. What was it? Ten, Jesse?"

"When you came to the village with Uncle Mirek? You were ten. I remember because you wanted to kiss Isabella behind the tree. I said you couldn't until she was ten, too."

"Ah, Isabella," he said, glancing over at the innkeeper's wife. She was putting down food onto a different table. He sighed as if in remembrance. Well, he'd had Isabella too, probably more times than me.

"You've known each other since you were ten? I guess that's why you trusted him to find you a wife," she said, watching me carefully to see how I would react to her comment.

"It's a little complicated," I said, not wanting to get into an involved conversation.

"No kidding. Apparently it's complicated enough that Porter can't tell me a damn thing about it. It's been three weeks!"

I wondered why Porter couldn't find me one without a potty mouth. I didn't say a word, but my expression must have revealed my feelings. She looked at me quickly.

"Oh, shit. I'm not supposed to swear, am I?"

Porter laughed. "It's not befitting a lady," I said.

"Why didn't you tell me before? You've been letting me swear the whole time," she said, frowning at Porter accusingly.

"It was cute," he said. "I didn't have the heart to tell you to stop."

She huffed out her breath, but I could tell she enjoyed his teasing. Of course she did. Porter had charmed my bride. Great. I never could compete with him with girls. Her eyes cut over to me, and she became serious again.

"I'm sorry. I'll stop it." But she looked like she wasn't sure she could. "I guess I'm not what you were expecting in a wife."

I looked at Porter. That was a loaded question. "Like I said, it's complicated."

"You didn't answer the question," she said, pointing at me with a spoon. Isabella had brought us some stew and more bread. "I've waited three weeks for the answer, so please don't make me wait any longer."

I sighed. "Fine. It's going to come out sooner or later. You might as well know that they've branded me. I'm a Renegade."

"A Renegade? What's that?" Porter shook his head when I looked at him.

"You must be aware that we have particular laws on our planet that ban the possession of certain things."

"Oh, yes. *Things*. I had to leave behind a lot of *things* before I beamed down. I heard about your *laws*."

The way she said laws made me think she didn't like them very much.

"When I was young and stupid, I found some prohibited items. Instead of turning them over to the authorities immediately, I kept them for a bit."

"You did?"

"Yes. It was foolish. I was tattooed with an **R** on my shoulder to mark me as a Renegade. It's what we call anyone who is misguided, messes around with things, and gets caught."

"I see. I don't agree with everything, but I think I understand."

51

"No woman in this village or any other will have me because of the incident," I said. "That's why I needed Porter's help to find me a bride. My father is ill, and I must inherit to ensure the farm stays in our family. To do that, I need a wife."

She looked at me. "That sucks."

I blinked at the unusual use of the word. Of course, we spoke Standard. Everyone does. It's the language used throughout the entire galaxy. However, since we had little contact with the outside universe, our version of Standard drifted and missed some vocabulary.

Sucks, like a baby hundinlark sucks at its mother's teats? She seemed to be implying I was having bad luck. That was partially true, but I had also made an incorrect decision which hadn't had much to do with luck, but everything to do with stupidity.

"He was lucky," Porter said. There was that word *luck* again. "It could have been a lot worse. They were lenient because he was only a boy."

"Sounds like they ruined your life." She turned to me with sympathetic eyes.

"At least he still has a life."

Porter was cut off then when a man came thundering down the stairs and into our room, heading out the door. Men in dark navy suits clattered down after him, one of them with a small sledgehammer over his shoulder, the other with a crossbow out and an arrow loaded. He was almost to the door when they started shouting.

"Bar the door. Don't let him escape."

Immediately, two patrons stepped between the fleeing man and the door. If they hadn't assisted the Bureau of Purity, they would have been in trouble themselves. No one crossed the Bureau. The poor soul skidded to a stop, and his eyes darted around as he looked for another escape route.

He didn't find anyone to help him. We couldn't. The two men grabbed him before he could get away.

Porter and I looked at each other in consternation. What were they doing this far out? My woman watched the confrontation with worry in her eyes. Porter ducked down under the table to hide, pretending he had dropped his fork.

The restrained man chose the only option he had left. He punched one of the Bureau men in the face and somehow spun out of their grasp. He made a break for the kitchen. I guess he hoped there would be an escape route for him.

The men from the Bureau had dropped their weapons in the scuffle. They grabbed their crossbows and went out the front door without saying anything. The rest of us spilled out after them, eager for a show. All of us except Porter. He remained hidden inside the building.

They split up, each going around one side of the building. In a moment, we all heard a scream. They came back dragging a body.

As they came closer to the crowd, I could see the man had an arrow in his back, straight through the heart. He was gasping, but it wouldn't be for long.

"I can't believe it," my fiancee whispered, her face appalled.

Well, that was the idea. Punish offenders completely so they wouldn't think of dissenting.

"This man possessed high technology items," they shouted. "When we tried to arrest him, he ran. He has received his punishment, and it was just."

I looked at the man. His eyes were glazed, and he had stopped breathing.

"Is he dead?" she whispered, her face white.

"He would have been executed eventually, even if they left him alive," I replied.

The other Bureau agent had been searching the body. Finally, he held up an offending device, threw it on the ground, and smashed it repeatedly with the sledgehammer until nothing remained but dust. We all watched in silence.

"Yordbrook will remain free from technology," one of the men spoke into the silence. "We will protect you from the evil. There will never be a return to the chaos that came after the bombs. We will protect you from all such things and the people who use and hide them."

In unison, we said, "Thank you."

The other man was struggling to hold the dead body from under its arms. They walked away, dragging it with them, heading for the wagons and carriages.

Now that the show was over, everyone turned away and resumed their activities. It would be something to talk about for days in a part of the planet where nothing exciting ever happened. I suspected the man was on the run, and they had finally caught up with him.

"Annalee?" I felt concerned. She appeared faint. "Are you all right?"

She shook her head. "Let's go back inside."

We found Porter upstairs in a room he had reserved for the next few days.

"I'll feel better if you talk," she said, looking back and forth between the two of us.

"We created the Bureau of Purity years after the catastrophe that marked the end of The Before Times," I said, telling the beginning of a story I had heard many times before.

"What catastrophe?"

Porter and I glanced at each other.

"We had a disaster. A war nearly destroyed everyone on Yordbrook. When our ancestors finished rebuilding afterward, they decided that if there wasn't any technology to create such destruction, everyone would be safe."

"Who were they?"

"That was the Bureau of Purity," I said, feeling nauseated. "They enforce the law, which usually means hunting down Renegades or members of the Underground and destroying their technology. They typically take Renegades back to the capital."

"Why did they kill him?" she asked, looking as if she might be sick to her stomach.

"Because he refused to go quietly."

"Would he have died anyway?"

I hesitated for a moment. "Yes. There's no need for a trial if they catch you possessing prohibited items. The only sentence is death," Porter said. I looked at her, rubbing my shoulder.

"But they were lenient with you," she said, frowning. I nodded. "Because you were underage. I'm beginning to think that being branded a Renegade and being shunned by your people was a blessing in disguise. What is this place doing to me?"

She looked around at the inn and the beautiful green fields beyond it. One of the suns had already descended under the horizon, and the other two were retreating as well. Except for the Bureau, Yordbrook was idyllic. I remembered the stories about The Before Times and how ugly the planet became.

In our time, no vehicles polluted the air with smoke or noise. No wires crisscrossed the sky. No buildings blocked out the suns. I had to admit that our ancestors had the right idea when they colonized the planet, but they hadn't gone about it the right way.

Annalee and I made our goodbyes quickly. We needed to get home.

Porter said he would see us at the wedding. I wondered why he was leaving so abruptly, but I could guess. Watching the Bureau of Purity at work always put me on edge as well.

"You're a dead man walking," she said thoughtfully.

"Pretty much. It was fortunate for me that I was underage at the time and they let me live. Most Renegades either reoffend or they join the Underground."

"What's that?"

"It's a rebel group that wants technology to be a regular part of life again for our people. They're not too creative with their naming, but they're excellent at hiding themselves. King Murtaugh, our current ruler, is efficient and brought the Bureau to their current level of effectiveness and cruelty."

"You still have a king?"

"We are a monarchy combined with a representative council. Each county has a voice, no matter how large or how small. The king and the council cooperate on most things."

"Does the Underground really risk their lives to try to bring technology back to your planet?"

"That's right."

"It sounds crazy. Those Bureau guys were brutal."

"People who volunteer for the Underground have to be a little messed up in the head," I said. "Let's go home now. Father is expecting us."

She nodded but froze when she spotted the blood in the dirt where the man had bled from his wound. I didn't know what she was thinking, but she looked terrified as she rubbed the back of her hand compulsively.

I was fortunate those drops of blood weren't mine. I was afraid too. The Bureau of Purity was no joke.

I definitely was crazy.

The question was, would the risks I took be worth it?

CHAPTER 5

JESSE

I led us up a corridor. My father lay dying at the end of it. As we entered, my heart clenched at the sight of him looking so frail.

"Jesse," he said weakly. "Who is this lovely young woman you have brought with you?"

Lovely? Was he joking?

I ignored the comment and got right to the point. He certainly didn't have any time left for beating around the bush.

"Her name is Annalee, Father. We're getting married."

His demeanor changed immediately. "Married?" His face lit up with happiness. "When and how did this happen?"

"Don't worry about the details, please, Father. Isn't it enough to know we will marry today?"

Annalee glanced at me quickly. Porter had filled me in on the stipulations of TerraMates. The couple was supposed to marry within twenty-four hours of the woman's arrival on the planet. But since Yordbrook had transportation issues and there was no way we could be together in less than three weeks, they were giving us a special dispensation.

"That is wonderful, Jesse. Where are you going to have the ceremony?"

"At the church, Father. We will get you there and in the front row. Don't worry."

"Of course. I would never miss it. I am fortunate to be here for your marriage, my son. And my daughter," he said, beaming at Annalee. She smiled back. It was an authentic smile, unlike the ones she had been giving me.

What was this nonsense about her being lovely? I studied her silently while she made small talk with my father about her trip. They seemed to get along well together. When she laughed, and her eyes sparkled, I couldn't help but smile, too.

But when she looked back at me, her face became grave again, and her aura disappeared. Once again I noticed her imperfections and how untidy she was. My father's eyesight was failing, along with the rest of his body. Despite our disagreement about my future wife, I was relieved to know he was still alive to see my wedding day. He would be able to die peacefully now.

"Come with me," I said, and she looked up at me with trepidation. "Mrs. Boyko will help you bathe and dress for the wedding. You will have some time to rest. We will marry in the evening."

"I will have the lawyers draw up the paperwork today, Jesse. As soon as the marriage is final, I will transfer the farm to your name and all our troubles will be over."

"Indeed, Father," I said. He beamed at me.

All I had to do was marry Annalee and the hard times would be behind us. It was the perfect solution.

ANNALEE

I was getting married, but this was not how I had imagined it when I was a girl.

I rubbed the back of my hand for comfort. My phone should have been there, but I had concealed it elsewhere. I looked around at all the strangers in the pews. Even my husband was an unknown element. The only person I felt a sense of kinship with was Mr. Melnyk, Jesse's father.

He had been kindness personified since I had met him and I was grateful he was here. There was one kindly face in a sea of stony expressions. I wasn't sure what the problem was. Maybe I wasn't a model bride. Maybe they didn't like off-worlders. Maybe they didn't like outsiders, period.

I had a vague sense of something odd at customs, but the more I interacted with the natives I was starting to realize their society was repressive in many ways.

The service passed by in a blur. I hardly noticed what was happening. I was tired and overwhelmed. It all seemed like a dream until I felt Jesse putting a ring on my finger and promising to love, honor, and protect me.

It was surprising, but I suppose he couldn't say, "I promise to marry you for a year." Marriage was meant to be forever. Wait, what had the minister just said?

A quiet stillness filled the church.

"Did he just say I had to promise to love, honor and obey you?" I whispered frantically to Jesse.

"Of course," he whispered back. "You do realize this is a wedding, don't you? Just say it, people are watching us."

"I'm not going to promise to obey you."

He looked incredulous. "There's no other way to get married on this planet. If you don't promise, everything stops."

"Can't he change the wording slightly?" I felt like the people around us could hear every word I was saying.

"No," he hissed. "He can't. You are embarrassing me. And my father." He added the last bit as an afterthought, and I thought it might be to incentivize me. His father was the only person whose feelings I wanted to consider here. If I were embarrassing Mr. Melnyk, I would have to swallow my pride. He had been kind to me and didn't deserve further aggravation.

I looked at the minister, who was watching the whispers in the middle of his ceremony with bemusement.

"I'm sorry, could you repeat that one more time?" I asked, and gave him a nervous smile.

"Do you, Miss Annalee Beauchene, promise to love, honor, and obey Mr. Jesse Melnyk?"

"I do," I shouted. Then I leaned in and whispered, "...as long as I agree with what he is ordering me to do."

His eyes bulged with indignation. I looked at him triumphantly. I thought I had evaded danger. I was not going to obey him like a slave.

How had I ever thought TerraMates was a good idea?

The rest of the wedding was a blur. We exchanged rings and signed some papers and suddenly it over. I felt the urge to take a picture of ourselves, but I managed to suppress it. Mr. Melnyk offered his congratulations to us while everyone else in the church filed out.

I couldn't help overhearing people's conversations about me. Maybe they wanted me to hear. People thought I was crazy or a bad person or both for marrying Jesse. I wondered what Porter had meant when he asked me not to judge him based on what other people thought.

That wasn't a problem. I wasn't judging him based on what other people thought. I was judging him by what he did and our interactions over the past twelve hours.

He was a jerk. An asshole. An inconsiderate wretch.

It felt good to call him a wretch. I didn't know the exact definition of the word, and I couldn't easily look up the meaning, but it felt like an appropriate description here. How could he expect me to obey him? I seethed over the idea until my rational mind offered an explanation for his behavior.

He probably expected it because the ceremony included things all women were supposed to promise on this planet. We weren't on Earth anymore. Still, I wasn't from

Yordbrook. I wasn't sure what or how much I was willing to change about myself.

For a moment, I felt trapped and terrified. What had I done to myself? I couldn't even leave this town without taking a three-week trip back to the station. If I managed to do that by myself, I would have to talk someone into beaming me back up. I had no idea how to do that because I had no money. I was stuck here for a year, no matter what.

My phone was now sewn securely into the hem of my dress, thanks to the needle and thread of a kindly innkeeper's wife. I hadn't had to leave all parts of my old life behind. And thank goodness I didn't have to sleep with him unless I wanted to. That was part of the TerraMates contract.

Then I had a terrible thought. Had Jesse signed it? After seeing the two of them together, I suspected Porter had organized my marriage himself. Jesse hadn't known I was his bride when he saw me, which meant he hadn't seen my profile picture.

If he didn't know about the restrictions on sex, I would have to tell him. But how would I do it? He seemed to love his father, and I could threaten to tell his father if he tried to force himself on me.

I thought back to my arrival and how he had looked before he opened his mouth and ruined my impression. I felt a tiny stirring of arousal from the memory. But he was too much of a jerk for the feeling to last. It didn't matter if the man was a sex god (and he looked like he might be one between the sheets). If he was an asshole, it was a big turn-off.

It was a good thing I wasn't thinking about the broad chest, bulging tattooed biceps, and the six-pack from heaven I caught a glimpse of earlier. The laundress had stopped him and asked if there were any other dirty clothes. Without thinking, he took off his shirt and threw it in her basket. By the look on her face, she was used to it. Maybe she had asked him on purpose to get a glimpse of him.

I guess it must be all the hard labor on the farm, but Jesse Melnyk had one sexy body.

I still couldn't reconcile his appearance with the way he treated me. If I didn't feel like I cared about him and he cared about me, there was no way I was sleeping with him.

We needed to talk about this as soon as possible. I didn't want him to think he was going to get it on and be disappointed when I turned him down. He would be frustrated and angry if that happened. I didn't know if Jesse was dangerous, and I didn't want to find out.

We walked out of the church, and Jesse helped me up into the carriage. I assumed he was only providing assistance because there were people around. The servants would ensure Mr. Melnyk got home safely. I sat as far away from him as I could. For the first time, I felt afraid. He hadn't displayed any kindness or interest to me.

What if he tried to abuse me? As far as I knew, TerraMates investigated all their applicants, but was that even possible on a world like Yordbrook?

"Why are you looking at me like that?" he said harshly.

I didn't answer because I didn't know what to say.

"Speak up. You've no need to fear me. I won't be a cruel husband."

Wouldn't he? I accidentally shook my head.

"You don't believe me? What kind of a person do you think I am? I've never harmed a girl or woman in my life, and I don't intend to start now." He looked at me in consternation. "Why don't you speak? You were talking enough in the middle of the ceremony," he said, his face sour.

When there was a moment of silence, I grabbed it. "I would speak if you gave me more than three seconds to answer you," I murmured. "How am I to know your disposition? I don't know you. You've been rude to me since I arrived. I'm starting to feel a little nervous that I married you."

He cut me off.

"You think I've been rude? And angry?" He was looking upset now.

"Yes," I told him directly. I might as well be clear.

He mulled the thought for a while. "Perhaps you're right," he said. "I apologize if I was."

"Thank you," I said, graciously.

We sat in awkward silence.

"I wish to be a good husband." He didn't look at me. "I may need assistance."

He had paused before the word assistance. I wondered if he had ever asked for help before. Jesse had given an inch. I supposed I could yield as well.

"I'll try. But I've never been a wife before. I might not know how to do it properly either."

He frowned. "Are you pure? I thought you had already lain with a man."

My eyes got wide. "Pure? Oh no. Why would you think that?"

"You said you didn't know how to do it properly. It was surprising because off-worlders are considered to be different. I mean, women from other planets are thought to be more experienced."

"More experienced in what?" I asked.

"Sexual things," he said.

"If you're asking if I'm a virgin, I'm not pure."

He didn't say anything and stared straight ahead.

I couldn't seem to stop myself from talking. "Not a lot, and only with one guy. It was a long time ago. It might feel like I'm pure." What was I saying? He was blushing again.

"Speaking of sex," I said, ignoring his discomfort. "TerraMates had a list of rules for the newlyweds. Did you happen to read it?"

"No," he shook his head. "Porter did it all."

"Did he forge your signature, too?" Jesse nodded. "Great," I said, huffing out my breath and crossing my arms over my chest. I stared off to the side of the carriage at the dark green foliage of the trees lining the road.

"Wait, what you mean by forge?"

"Someone signed a contract. Either you or Porter did, I guess."

"I gave him a letter that said he was acting on my behalf. Everything's legal. Don't worry," he said.

I was surprised, though I shouldn't have been.

"But what were you saying about lying together?"

"We only lie together if we both agree. If I don't want to have sex with you, I don't have to."

"But we must consummate the marriage," he insisted.

"Says who?"

69

"Otherwise, the ceremony is not official."

"What?" The marriage had to be binding, or I wouldn't get the money to go to school and become a teacher. I saw my dreams going down in flames and started to realize I would have to make sacrifices if I wanted to achieve them.

"We'll say we did it," I said. "No problem."

He looked embarrassed. "There'll be a witness to verify the activities."

"A witness?" I was shouting now.

"They won't be in the room."

"Where are they going to be, then?"

"Usually, they wait in the hall or downstairs at the inn. They'll be able to confirm we consummate the marriage."

I started to laugh nervously. "And how do they confirm it?"

Jesse shrugged. Apparently, he didn't want to tell me. That couldn't be good.

"At this point, I have no desire to lie with you," I said, flashing him an irritated look.

He studied my face for a moment and finally let a smile appear on his face. It was dazzling. It was the first time I saw genuine emotion on his face, and he was incredibly attractive when he smiled.

I caught my breath. Had I just said I didn't want to sleep with him? What was I, stupid or something?

"Perhaps I can change your mind," he said huskily. For a moment, his blue eyes appeared smoky and made my breath accelerate.

Had Jesse been holding out on me? Did he save up his charm and only release it when needed? Well, I was good at resisting attractive guys. Many of them had tried to take me home when I was working the late shift at the fancy restaurant back home. Some of them had been handsome and extremely persuasive.

At the time, I had integrity, a plan, and a dream. Also, I had a job the next morning.

Maybe I had been scared of letting any of them get close to me.

Now everything was different from Earth. I had married Jesse. We were going to be living as husband and wife for a year until I requested my divorce and TerraMates helped me get it quickly and quietly, just as they promised in their paperwork. I would head back to Earth to register for my bachelor of education degree. In five years, I would become a full-fledged teacher, living my dream life.

I wasn't worried about work the next morning right now.

He looked to the front and called out a command to turn into the yard. He still radiated sexuality, and I told myself that I could resist him. Especially if he was going to continue being a jerk. I hoped I wouldn't let myself sleep with an asshole.

When we pulled in, he came around, offering his hand. "Thanks," I said, taking it and stepping out. His hand was warm and firm. I felt my face flush as my body tingled where he touched me. Resisting my husband was going to be harder than I had originally thought. He dropped my hand, and we walked toward the house.

"Jesse?" I said, looking as innocent as possible.

"Yes?" he said, turning his head to look at me.

"In case you feel the need to address me directly, my name is Annalee."

His face got red. "Indeed," he said, as we reached the house. A servant opened the door for us. He glanced sideways again and gave me a look that sent shivers through my body. "Welcome to the Melnyk homestead, Annalee. Our home is your home."

CHAPTER 6

JESSE

I stood by the bar and watched as my new wife, Annalee, held my father's hands and danced with him where he sat in his chair. If she had tried to do anything on purpose that would get her into my good books, it would have been to honor my father.

I felt myself softening towards her as I watched her enjoy her time with him. He had already told me twice how lucky I was to have found such a gem. I didn't agree with his assessment, but she was becoming less annoying.

When the music changed, Porter walked over and spoke to Annalee. She smiled at him with a light in her eyes that didn't shine for me. He pulled her into his arms and whirled around the room, barely avoiding a crash into the other dancing couples. The warmth I felt towards her disappeared abruptly.

They spun madly in circles. Annalee threw her head back, laughing, and Porter grinned from ear to ear. He had no right to be making my bride laugh like that. She should only laugh for me.

The inn's doors opened, and two men wearing dark clothes entered the room. I wondered who they were. Myron walked over to the pair, hopefully intending to tell them this was a private party.

As the men turned around, I caught sight of their faces. The men were from the Bureau of Purity. Why were they here? My eyes flickered to where I had last seen Porter, but he had vanished.

One of the Bureau agents scanned the room, and his gaze stopped on me. He lingered for a moment. I felt myself start to sweat. Thankfully they nodded and walked out.

Everyone thought they had gone back to the city after they murdered their potential offender. I didn't have anything for them to find, but they would make anyone worried.

I noticed my father beckoning to me from across the room, and I went to him quickly, hoping everything was all right. I wondered if seeing the Bureau of Purity men had upset him.

"Jesse, my boy," he said, giving me a sympathetic look as I crouched down beside his chair so he could look me in the eyes. "Stop scowling at your wife. If you don't want your friend charming your bride, go and get her. She's yours now. Not his."

He wasn't upset about the Bureau of Purity men at all. He was concerned about me. My father was the kindest man you could ever meet. Watching him die a slow death was painful, but there was nothing I could do for him. I felt a suffocating feeling in my chest every time I thought about his future.

"She doesn't want to dance with me," I said, staring at the floor.

"That's because you're glowering at her. Try putting a smile on your face, boy. You look like you're at a funeral, not your wedding. I know this isn't the usual situation, but you'd be surprised at how many people are surprised by each other after they get married. She's a wonderful lass, Jesse. She could be good for you if you give her a chance."

"Of course I'll give her a chance!"

"Right," my father said, giving me a skeptical look. "You're just waiting for the right opportunity, aren't you?"

"I've given her a chance," I said, exhaling and searching the room for Annalee. She and Porter were sitting at a table together and drinking wine.

She looked like she was flirting shamelessly with Porter, which made me upset. I hoped there wasn't any morelia involved.

The substance was illegal. Many an unscrupulous man had used it to get a woman into bed when she wasn't the least bit interested in him. Someone was still growing it. Morelia was available for purchase if you knew where to find it.

I didn't mind if the woman took it voluntarily, but it made me sick to my stomach when I imagined using it on someone who was unwilling. I hoped no one had brought any here tonight.

"You haven't given her the slightest chance," my father said, shaking his head at me. "Go and dance with your wife. Be your naturally charming self, Jesse. Goodness knows you're handsome enough to woo any woman. Annalee is willing if you make the effort."

He looked at me with a sad expression in his eyes. I didn't want to disappoint my father, especially if we only had a little time left together.

I would do well to listen to his advice. He and my mother had been deliriously happy together my whole life until she passed away. He knew what he was talking about when it came to relationships. Then again, he and my mother had been in love, so the cards were stacked in their favor from the beginning.

"How about this? Pretend she's a beautiful girl you've seen at an inn when you're out with friends. Go and talk to her. Ask her to dance. Pay attention to her, and you'll be well on your way to a happy marriage, son."

"Yes, Father," I said, waving my hand from my head to his as a gesture of love and respect. I rose and walked across the room. I hoped this wasn't going to be a hard thing to do. I had approached many girls over the course of my life. Most had been more than happy to receive my attention.

Annalee looked up from her conversation with Porter as I approached and the smile fell from her face. She swallowed and looked down at the floor. Was I already screwing this up?

"Hey, Jess," Porter said, sounding a little too jovial. He had been drinking the free-flowing wine and ale and was intoxicated. His expression turned uncomfortable.

"I just had a dance with Annalee, and she's been begging me for another, but you know how my knee gets."

I did. He injured it in a carriage accident years ago and it had never been the same. I was sure he wasn't feeling much pain now considering the amount of alcohol in his system. Still, he was giving me an opening, and I would take it.

"Would you like to dance, Annalee?"

Her name felt strange on my lips. She noticed I used her name, but I also sensed she knew I felt uncomfortable with it. I was trying too hard.

"Sure," she said with a forced smile. "What are weddings without dancing?"

Porter smiled at us hopefully, raising his glass to me and then turning away.

It was time to extinguish any rumors. People had been giving me strange looks because the bride was dancing so much with the best man and not the groom. I wouldn't have Annalee's good name besmirched by nasty gossip.

"Indeed," I said, pulling her to me. As I tapped my foot to the beat, I began to whirl her around the floor. Soon she was laughing as we linked arms and moved between two rows of couples. When we got to the end of the line and lifted our hands to join them, becoming part of an arch, I felt my fingers tingle as they touched hers.

I smiled again, and her eyes softened. Maybe tonight would be fun after all.

ANNALEE

After the last couple had swept down between two rows of people facing each other, each man and woman began to dance with their partner again. Jesse pulled me in close, and I felt my whole body catch fire in a way it hadn't with Porter.

Porter was charming and handsome. He was kind to me. I guess I had a slight crush on him. But Jesse was another story altogether. He made me angry and scared. Right now I was filled with lust. He smelled good, and he was a ridiculously good dancer, which surprised me. It seemed that, on this planet, the men danced as often as the women. It was a pleasant change from the *I'm-too-cool-to-dance* attitude of many of the men I knew back on Earth.

As I stared into my husband's eyes, I reminded myself that he wasn't exactly a man. The thought gave me a naughty thrill.

"What are you thinking of, wife?" Jesse said, his eyes smoldering.

I didn't know what to say, but I certainly wasn't going to tell him I thought he was an alien, and it was turning me on.

"I'm thinking about what happens next," I said, trying not to blush. That was true, wasn't it? I was thinking of the night and what he would do to me when we were supposed to consummate the marriage.

I wasn't going to sleep with him, was I?

My body wanted to, and if the hardness I felt pressing up against me was any indication, his body wanted mine as well. I supposed that was good. If he could be less of a jerk, maybe my mind would feel like sleeping with him as well as my body.

The music changed, and he pressed himself against me, taking my hands and putting them on his shoulders. His hands dropped to my hips, pulling me tightly against his body.

"This is the bride and groom's dance," he said.

"I see."

"And it involves our bodies pressed firmly against each other," he said, somehow decreasing the distance between our bodies even though I hadn't thought it possible. People circled us and began to sing lyrics along with a slow, sweet melody played on one of the stringed instruments.

I stared up into his eyes. To my surprise, he planted a kiss on my forehead. The gesture was sweet and kind. My heart lurched and my eyes filled with tears. It was the first sign that he might eventually come to care about me, and it gave me hope.

Soon the people in the circle stopped swaying and began clapping and stomping their feet, taking the tempo up a little bit at a time and singing more quickly. Jesse had one hand around my waist, and the other held my hand. He was rapidly dancing with me around the circle.

At some point, he broke through it. I thought we were going to crash into the crowd, but they moved aside at the last minute to let us through.

Everyone burst into applause. Jesse smiled down at me with a look of happiness on his face.

"It's the first ritual. They expect me to kiss you," he said. The next thing I knew, he captured my lips. The kiss started out chaste, but before I realized what was happening, we had our arms wrapped around each other, and he was taking my breath away.

I vaguely heard the crowd hooting and yelling around us, but I lost myself in Jesse's touch, and I couldn't think clearly. I didn't care that a hundred people were witnessing our first kiss. All I cared about was him not stopping.

Eventually, it had to end. Thank goodness for the crowd noise because I think I slightly whimpered when he pulled away. He stared down at me, and I wondered what he was thinking.

There was no time to ask because Jesse's father was making a toast to the happy couple — I supposed that was us — and Jesse was ushering me out of the building. People went ahead of us tossing seeds on the ground before us to make us fertile.

I was thankful for the TerraMates birth control shot that ensured we would certainly not be fertile. Jesse hadn't had his shot, but I certainly had mine, and I was glad for it. I wouldn't get pregnant in my year on the planet. No one here would know why. They'd think we hadn't been lucky enough to have a baby, which was fine with me.

.

When the crowd dissipated, we were left to walk the rest of the way alone. We were silent, and I felt uncomfortable again. Suddenly we heard a shout from behind us. It was Porter.

"I didn't get to wish you well," he said. "I'm leaving in the morning so I won't be seeing you."

Jesse frowned. "Why are you leaving so soon?"

"Let's just say the Bureau of Purity makes me nervous," he said, not looking nervous at all. Porter took my hand and kissed it.

"You aren't the only one," Jesse said, cryptically. I supposed he meant the Bureau of Purity made everyone nervous. They certainly made me feel uncomfortable now that I had seen them in action.

"I wish you both the best," Porter said. "Might have a word with Jesse in private?"

He smiled graciously at me. I walked slightly ahead while they dropped behind. I took the opportunity to make sure my phone was still in the hem of my skirt. After Jesse had fucked me — it would probably take only minutes — I would find a private place to look at my pictures.

When I looked back, the men were having a heated discussion. What could Porter have to say to Jesse that he wouldn't want to say in front of me? They appeared to be talking about a grave matter by the looks on their faces. Porter produced a small bottle of something that made Jesse react violently.

He pushed it away and looked around furtively as if he didn't want to be seen with Porter or the bottle. Porter tried to press the bottle on him, but Jesse shook his head again. Porter opened his arms to give Jesse a hug, and I saw him surreptitiously slip the tiny bottle into Jesse's coat pocket. Jesse patted Porter on the back before they separated.

Porter waved at me and then vanished. Suddenly Jesse was coming toward me with a look in his eyes that made me weak in the knees and a little wet between the legs. I didn't think I was ready. There was no emotional connection between us.

My body was screaming *To hell with emotional connection, just screw him already!*

What I didn't like was my lack of choice in the matter. He said we had to consummate the marriage, and there would be a witness.

Although we didn't talk for the rest of the walk, I was aware of every move he made. His hand brushed my hand several times making energy explode through my body. Even if my morals were doing a good job convincing me I shouldn't sleep with an alien I just met, my libido was doing just as good a job of blindfolding my morals and tying them up. It wanted to have fun tonight.

We got back to Jesse's homestead. He led me to a cabin where the older generation usually lived. The younger couple often lived in the house. Since Jesse's grandparents were deceased, we were going to live there temporarily.

He nodded to a man leaning against the side of the house. The witness, I supposed. I thought I would be disgusted, but it a strange way it made me excited to imagine someone listening to me. Maybe I was more of a bad girl than I imagined, and I simply needed the right situation to unleash it.

All the sex back home had been nice, but I had no desire to repeat it. I had done it because I wanted to be closer to my boyfriend, not because of the ecstasy he brought me. As I glanced over at the Adonis beside me, all muscles and pure testosterone, I thought perhaps tonight might be different. I shivered at the thought.

CHAPTER 7

ANNALEE

After Jesse opened the door, he had a question for me. "Do you remember what to do now?"

I nodded. I had been given the crash course in newlywed Yordbrook customs by a kind female servant, Mrs. Boyko, who worked for Jesse's father.

He stepped through the door, and I stood outside, waiting. He reached his hand to me. I took it, making sure my eyes never left his.

"Will you come in, wife?" he asked, his voice deepening and sounding rough. The question seemed innocent but was supposed to symbolize him inviting me into his life and his family.

My acquiescence implied agreeing to love, honor, and obey him (as long as I agreed with what he was asking me to do). It was an admission that I would sleep with him and bear his children.

We weren't having a Vegas wedding with a divorce lawyer waiting for me at the end of the year, ready to invalidate everything. At the moment, it felt serious. He meant what he was saying.

Here on Yordbrook, the act of me stepping over the threshold made my marriage legally binding. Well, that and him fucking me. Jesse would have a lot of control over my life.

I stared at him, suddenly unsure if I could do it. Could I give myself into this man's hands? I didn't know him. I wasn't sure if I liked him. And I certainly didn't trust him.

But what else was I going to do? If I hadn't wanted to marry a stranger, then I shouldn't have signed up for TerraMates. There was no turning back now. All these thoughts flew through my head in the blink of an eye, and I confidently lifted my head.

"I will," I answered, stepping into the cabin. Before I could place my foot on the floor of the house, he pulled me into his arms and started kissing me senseless.

That was part of the ritual, too, indicating the man accepted his wife's surrender.

As he kissed me, I thought that if the sex were as good as it promised to be, this marriage thing wouldn't be terrible. I was of two minds about sleeping with him. One part of me wanted to lie down and spread my legs. The other cautioned me to be prudent, wait, and keep my knees together like I had been taught.

He set me down, and I looked around the room. "I will visit the privy," he whispered in my ear, making me shiver at the sensation. "Then you may, and we will consummate the marriage. There must be no doubt, or I will not be allowed to inherit. You understand?"

I nodded. Mrs. Boyko had explained everything to me. I wasn't going to mess anything up despite my earlier misgivings. I had to hold onto my dream through all the madness of a strange backward culture. My discomfort would be temporary.

He took off his coat and laid it on a chair, then went back out the door to the composting toilet. At least I wasn't stuck somewhere with outhouses. The stink would have driven me back to Earth in the first week. I almost looked forward to using the fragrant composting toilets that smelled of fresh wood shavings. We covered our business with leaves from the forest floor.

I walked around the room, nervously trailing my hand along the table, on the back of the chair, then over Jesse's coat which promptly fell to the floor with a thump. I bent over to pick it up and dusted it off. Something fell out of the pocket.

The bottle was unmarked. Porter had probably given him a strong drink to enhance his courage. Did Jesse need courage? Maybe it was to prevent Jesse from noticing my plain looks.

I winced. Damn. Maybe I needed alcohol to give *me* some courage. If I were a little drunk, it wouldn't be difficult to sleep with someone I barely knew.

Before I could think too much about it, I had the cap off and tipped the bottle into my mouth. The taste was pleasant, and I felt it going straight to my head. I took three or four more pulls and felt pleasantly buzzed. This was a good idea, right?

I heard Jesse's feet crunching on the gravel as he came back up the path and I fumbled with the lid. For some reason, I wasn't as coordinated as I had been a few minutes ago. I managed to get the lid on and the bottle back in his pocket just as he walked in the door.

He looked at me putting his coat back on the chair without any expression on his face. I felt nervous and patted the jacket.

"It fell over," I explained unnecessarily.

"Why do you look as if I've caught you with your hand in the sugar?"

"I don't know what you're talking about."

He didn't look convinced but didn't pursue it. "Perhaps you'd like to visit the privy before we get started?"

I felt my heart begin to pound at the thought of getting started. I nodded eagerly and walked as quickly as I could to the bathroom. I couldn't help but wonder what Jesse would look like naked. I felt my nipples harden under my clothes, and my breath came faster.

I was getting horny. I could feel how wet I was between my legs. If they wore panties on this planet, mine would be soaked by now. Since they didn't, I knew I was getting slick.

By the time I returned to the house, I felt flushed and needy. Jesse looked at me with a funny look in his eyes.

"Are you all right?" he asked, his eyebrows pulling together.

Something pulled me towards him. I went to him and wrapped my arms around his neck.

"What is this?" he asked. When my lips covered his, he didn't say anything more, and only kissed me back.

After a lot of kissing, which involved a fair amount of tongue and hands roaming over our skin, Jesse pulled back. "What's come over you, Annalee?" he breathed.

"Nothing," I said. "I want you, Jesse. Badly."

He walked over to the table and sat down slowly in one of the chairs, putting his face in his hands.

"Are you okay?" I said, confused.

His voice came out from under his palms.

"Annalee?"

"Yes," I said, walking over to him, not sure what I had done wrong, but knowing I needed him to kiss me again. And touch me. And do very naughty things to me. I began rubbing his shoulders, making sure my breasts brushed against his back.

"Did you drink something since we got here?"

"I might have," I said.

"Was it from a bottle in my pocket?" he said, his eyes squinting a little in dismay. He pulled it out and shook it, inspecting the remaining liquid. Jesse raised his eyebrows.

"So what if I did?" I asked, feeling defensive. I liked the buzz, and I was feeling pretty good. "Give it to me. I want some more."

"No way," he said forcefully. I continued to reach for the bottle. "I wish you hadn't drunk any of it."

The way he said it made me instantly apprehensive, but did nothing to keep me from wanting to drink some more and needing Jesse more than anything.

"Why?"

"It's morelia," he sighed, dropping his eyes. "Porter wanted me to give some of it to you, but I refused. Morelia has a peculiar effect on women."

I waited.

Jesse looked uncomfortable. "It makes them want to lie with a man."

"That was not what I was expecting you to say," I said.

"Men sometimes use it in awful ways. It's illegal, but Porter thought it would make it easier for us this evening."

That reminded me that I was a woman, and I had needs.

"I can't undrink it, and I want some more, so could you hand it over?" I made a quick grab and snatched it out of his hand, running to the other side of the room as I uncapped it. I had it on my lips and swallowed the last of it before he knew what was happening.

"What are you doing?" he groaned, coming over to me. By then it was too late. He took the empty bottle out of my fingers as I began to feel the effects of the entire dose.

"Whoa," I said, swaying towards him. "You are fucking handsome, you alien man."

He rolled his eyes. I smiled broadly and pulled my hood back from my head. My long brown hair came tumbling down after I removed the pins. I began to unbutton my clothes but my fingers fumbled immediately.

Jesse shook his head and started to undress me quickly and efficiently. Soon I was only wearing my shift. The nipples on my large, round breasts stood out against the sheer, nearly transparent fabric. I thought I might start to drip if I got any wetter. Jesse needed to get inside me.

"You need to know everything about the morelia," he said, tucking a strand of hair behind my ear. The gesture was sweet and made me suck in my breath, causing me to inhale his scent. Jesse was still standing close beside me. His aroma increased the amount of pheromones I had in my system and made me even more horny.

We hadn't even touched yet.

"I don't care," I said. I managed to get one of his buttons undone. It was bigger than mine, and I was determined. I certainly hadn't been capable of undoing the tiny buttons on my dress. I worked away on the second one. There were only four total and then I would be able to touch his chest. I longed to get my hands on him — everywhere.

"I'm going to tell you," he said, letting me have my way with the buttons. He began a lecture as if we were in a school room. "Morelia is an addictive substance that creates an effect similar to becoming drunk. For instance, poor motor control." He looked at me pointedly. I ignored him, intent on unclasping the button and getting him naked. He droned on.

"It also makes the woman who ingests it want to mate with any man that she encounters."

"Any man?" I said, slightly appalled.

"Any man. That's why we banned it. She experiences an increased libido the more she drinks."

"Amen to that," I said, rubbing my sticky thighs together and exclaiming in satisfaction as I got another button undone.

"Also..." he hesitated again. The tone of his voice made me look up.

"You're not embarrassed, are you? I'm sure you've had women who were on morelia before," I said.

"Of course I have." I must have seemed surprised because he hastily added. "I never gave it to them."

"What do you mean?" I asked, cursing under my breath at the difficulty of getting the third button undone.

"Women will often take it themselves."

"What?" I said, giving a push. The third button popped out of its buttonhole. "Why would any woman in her right mind do that?"

"It assures the woman's orgasm. And..."

"There's more? In my book, anything that will guarantee the female orgasm in my book is the nectar of the fucking gods."

Although he had been offended before, now he seemed amused by my swearing.

"Not only does it assure her orgasm, but in my experience, it is an ecstatic one."

He hesitated. "And what? There's more? It can't be that bad."

"It's not bad. The women I've been with seem to like it well enough. The orgasm is strongest during penetration. The women are usually pretty loud, too."

I stopped work on the fourth button to look up at him. "It makes the woman horny and likely to have a mind-blowing orgasm while fucking? Morelia is an excellent drink. Is there more?"

I looked around as if expecting something to materialize suddenly on the table.

"What's so amazing about it?" he wondered, staring at me like he wanted to know how my crazy mind worked.

"Do you know how many women on Earth want something that could make them more interested in sex and guaranteed an orgasm? It solves all the female sex problems."

"I didn't know women had any problems," Jesse said off-handedly.

"You poor, innocent man," I said, putting my hand on his cheek. "Have you only had women who were on morelia? Orgasm isn't a sure thing for a woman, especially if it's supposed to happen through a few seconds of thrusting, which, in fact, can make us uninterested in sex."

"A few seconds of thrusting?" He looked insulted.

"Okay, okay. A few minutes. Although two is generous for some guys."

He pulled me in and kissed me intensely, then drew back and bit his lip. "I'm not sure we should do this. Do I have your consent if you're on morelia?"

I tilted my head back to look at the ceiling. "I thought we had to consummate this thing no matter what," I said. "We want no doubt that the marriage was binding." I paused. "I have a confession to make. If it makes you feel better, I've been fantasizing about you all night. I would have slept with you even if I hadn't drunk a magic potion."

He looked at me intently. "Really?"

"Really. I also thought we wanted the guy outside to hear moans of bliss," I said, waggling my eyebrows at him.

If we didn't stop talking and start having sex, I was going to explode from desire.

"It should be screams of bliss," he muttered, undoing the fourth button and taking off his shirt.

"Let's do it," I said, my lips curving into a smile as I let my hands move over the muscles of his perfect chest.

He picked me up and carried me to the bedroom.

CHAPTER 8

JESSE

I couldn't keep my hands off the sexy little wench any longer. Something was turning me on. I didn't know if it was the ale, her smart mouth, or her fearlessness.

Her big juicy breasts that I could barely see through the thin material of her shift were driving me wild. I needed to touch them and taste them. I wanted to do everything to this woman. The morelia she had consumed should last until midnight, giving me plenty of time to do it all.

Right now, I could see she was reaching the point where her unsatisfied desire would begin making her uncomfortable to the point of pain. I didn't want that. It would be better to satisfy her right away.

I laid her down on the bed and covered her with my body, kissing her sweet lips and twining my tongue with hers. I wanted to possess her. She would know she was mine. Her body was mine. Her pleasure was mine and would come from me. Every bit of her was mine.

Even if it wasn't true, I wanted it to be, even if it was only for tonight.

She broke our kiss to beg.

"Please Jesse," she said, squirming and writhing beneath me. She needed me to touch her. It was time. I stripped the rest of our clothes off, and we lay naked on the covers of the bed during the hot summer evening. A sultry breeze blew through the open window, making the curtains billow.

I took one of her large breasts into my hand. "Oh yes," she gasped.

Then I had them both, and I was massaging and tweaking the nipples, making her squeal. She had her legs wrapped around mine. I could feel she was already extremely wet. I couldn't wait to sink into her hot, warm body.

But not yet. I bent my head and kissed around one nipple. She shivered and her breath was ragged. Then I licked it and blew. She sucked in air through her teeth. Finally, I gave her what I knew she needed.

My mouth closed over the hard bud, and she moaned. If I had known she was like this in bed, I wouldn't have been cold to her all day. I sucked, then kissed my way over to the other one, flicking it with my tongue until I couldn't wait any longer and closed my lips on it. She arched her back and clamped her legs around mine.

"Jesse," she whispered. "I can't wait any longer. I need you inside me."

What was a man to do when a woman said that? I had to satisfy her. She spread her legs wide for me, and I moved between them, ready to penetrate her the way she desired.

ANNALEE

"Please, Jesse." He was teasing my entrance. "I need it now."

He didn't keep me waiting a moment longer but pushed inside. Oh fuck, yeah. That was what I needed so badly. He probably wasn't huge but I was tight, so he certainly felt big. He pushed in further, and my eyes rolled back in my head.

"More," I groaned through my teeth.

"I don't want to hurt you, Ann."

"You won't hurt me."

He wouldn't hurry. He pressed his cock deeply into me, inch by inch, until I had taken all of him. When our hips were touching, he stopped and rested his forehead on me. We lay there feeling the exquisite sensations.

Finally, though, I felt as though I couldn't bear it if he didn't move. As if he had read my mind, he started to shift. Pulling out and thrusting back in, forcing a groan out of me. I wrapped my legs around him.

He drove into me methodically, and I felt an orgasm rising, the likes of which I had never known. Heat spread starting from my core and moving outward, making my skin hot and sweat burst out all over me. The pleasure intensified until the slightest touch from him was unbearable. If my nipple brushed his chest, or he kissed me, or he plunged in and out of me...anything and everything brought me closer and closer to the edge.

"Ann," he gasped. "I need to move quickly."

"Go ahead," I said. I knew it was what I needed, too.

He sped up, and I felt him rubbing a spot inside me that I didn't know existed. It seemed as if all the pleasure was coming from a single point in my body. Once he began driving into me with such speed, I shot over the edge. The explosion of pleasure was so intense that I cried out his name.

He continued to thrust into me as spasms wracked my body. After a minute I felt him stiffen and spill his seed inside me, filling me up. I had never had a guy come inside me before — without protection, I mean — and it was incredible. It was nothing like my last boyfriend's sad little pull-out and spurt into the condom.

Jesse was clearly a man — alien or not — and he had just given me the most incredible sexual experience of my life. My orgasm went on and on until I felt completely drained. Finally, I collapsed beneath his body. He was quiet as he lay over me. His body was relaxed, but he was putting most of his weight on his arms. Then he lifted his head. His startlingly blue eyes stared into my own.

I had to admit that I loved feeling him in and on and all around me. Being surrounded by Jesse was intoxicating. It made me want him again.

How could I want him again? We had just finished. But I did. And it wasn't the morelia. I was afraid that I simply desired him, and I wondered if my need would never stop.

JESSE

I woke once with Ann on top of me. Another time, I took her slow and sweet with me behind her. We were both on our sides. Each time was amazing and blew my mind.

As the gray dawn slipped into our bedroom, I opened my eyes, which felt heavy from lack of sleep. I didn't move because Ann was sleeping on my chest. Her soft, warm body curled against me. She looked exhausted but content, like she'd been well fucked.

She felt me move against her and rubbed herself along my body. She couldn't want more, could she? I felt myself responding to her touch and soon I was hard again. How could this be? Usually, I was in and out. I had planned to consummate our marriage and retire to the couch.

Instead, I had made love to her three times and was about to do it again. I didn't have any more time to think about it because she was spreading her legs for me again and I was sliding into her, amazed that it felt so good. It was a feeling I hadn't had for a long time. It was like coming home.

She didn't say a word. She closed her eyes and moved with me. Our bodies fit together perfectly. It surprised me because I would never have guessed it the first time I saw her. I noticed her skin turning pink in the candlelight, a sign that her climax was building. In moments, her breaths started coming faster. I watched her face, increasing the pace of my thrusting. Her body arched up to me, and I moved deep within her.

"Jesse," she whispered. I took a nipple into my mouth, sucking hard, then switched to the other one as she groaned and pressed her big, soft breast up into my mouth.

I drove into her more quickly.

"Look at me, Ann," I said, wanting to see her eyes.

She opened them slowly, as if she were coming back from a far-away place. I swallowed. I didn't know what I saw in her eyes, but I knew it was reflected in mine.

I leaned down, unable to stop myself. I kissed her deeply, twisting a nipple at the same time. She came instantly. The feeling of her clenching around me as I plunged in and out of her hot wetness sent me over the edge. I groaned, stiffening, as I emptied myself into her. Her orgasm was still going. She looked beautiful.

A few minutes later, when we lay curled up together, I realized I had a significantly different opinion of her beauty yesterday. What was going on with me?

"Jesse?" She lifted her head to look into my eyes.

"Mm, hm." My hand was tracing lazy circles on her back.

"I guess morelia is a crazy aphrodisiac, huh?"

She smiled, but I drew my eyebrows together, counting to myself.

"Even the largest dose of morelia can only last four hours. The body will clear it out by then, no matter how much you drink."

"Four hours," she said, frowning. "But that means it would have passed through my body at around twelve or one in the morning. We've done it at least..."

"Twice since then?" I said. "Yes, that's right." I shrugged. "I guess we're good together in bed."

"You guess we're good together?" She didn't believe what I was saying. Her eyebrows nearly touched her hairline. "If the morelia wore off long ago, good is not how I would describe it."

"How would you describe it?" "How would you describe it?" I knew I was fishing for compliments but I couldn't help it.

"Amazing, incredible, mind-blowing, like nothing I've ever experienced before."

"And that was after the morelia wore off?"

She nodded.

"I haven't had many women who weren't under the influence of morelia, so I guess I did okay."

She shook her head at me. "You heard the sounds I was making, right? I can't make that shit up." She frowned as if hearing herself swear for the first time. "I mean, I can't make that stuff up."

"Humble's not a word people usually use to describe me."

"Maybe I'm seeing another side of you," she said, looking as if the idea intrigued her.

I sat upright, suddenly remembering all the work that was waiting for me. It was the busy season for the farm, and everyone had to pitch in. It was time to rise.

"Where are you going?" she said, surprised.

"I need to do work. You may have another day or two off, but after that, you must start to learn some new skills. Mrs. Boyko will teach you everything you need to know. "

"I thought the servants did the work here," she said. She didn't look dismayed at the idea of working, but she was trying to understand life on my planet.

"The servants help with the work, but we share it equally. It is my understanding that on Earth, some types of work are better than others but that isn't the case here. The owner of the farm works as hard as his stable boy. Neither is considered better than the other."

"Nice. So I'm going to work, probably as much as Mrs. Boyko."

"You would be hard-pressed to work that hard, but that's the idea."

"I got it. I put in long hours back home, too. It's nothing new to me."

"You did?"

She nodded, sitting up. I was momentarily distracted by her lush breasts before she pulled the sheet up to cover them.

"I don't need two days off. I can start today. I have more energy here than on Earth. I sleep well, and I haven't been working, so I'm all rested up and ready to go."

I nodded, pulling on my shirt, which hung on a chair next to the bed. She had certainly been energetic last night.

She held up two fingers. "I had two jobs back home. That was enough to pay for my mom's life, and I was able to save enough to go to school and become a teacher.

"You were the one who earned the money to care for your mother?" he asked, a little surprised.

"During the day I would take care of three and four-year-olds, teaching them. At night, I would wait tables, like the woman you and Porter were ogling when I arrived."

"I wasn't ogling her," I said, drawing my eyebrows together. *How had she noticed?*

"Yes, you were," she said, giving me a glance that indicated she had seen right through me.

"It's good you know how to work. It will make your transition easier." I patted her thigh and got up to find my pants.

"So will spending the nights in your bed," she muttered. I didn't know if she meant me to hear, but I liked it.

Some time later, we were sitting in the kitchen. Our knees touched under the table. Mrs. Boyko was serving us some gruel.

I had helped Annalee get dressed. It would take a while for her to learn how to put on her clothing. She had cursed her outfit in an unfeminine way, but today I found her language amusing. What had happened to me? Was I truly besotted with this girl within a day?

It was evident that everyone was glad Annalee was here. I supposed I was too. The staff was up and bustling about, having breakfast and discussing what work should be done on the farm today. The women wished her good morning and the men made jokes about how she had slept, making her blush.

Our appearance, coupled with the sounds that came from the guest house all night long, ensured the marriage was binding. I had already confirmed the witness had signed the papers, making everything legal.

In the morning, Father's lawyers had come to transfer the deed to my name. My father was relieved to know I had inherited the farm.

We all looked up when we heard the sound of horses galloping into the yard. One of the stable lads went to see who had arrived. Annalee looked at me curiously, and I shrugged, continuing to eat my breakfast.

The door flew open without warning. The same men from the Bureau of Purity we had seen at the inn burst into the room. Mrs. Boyko frowned. "What do you think you're doing?" she said. "Coming into a house in that way? Shame on you. Haven't your mothers taught you manners?"

"They're from the Bureau of Purity, Mrs. Boyko," I said, standing slowly. Annalee looked terrified.

"I don't care where they're from. There's such a thing as knocking," she said indignantly. I noticed she looked slightly whiter, and her voice was weaker than before.

"We are here to perform a search," one of the agents said. "Who is the man of the house?" I noticed Annalee's eyes roll but ignored them.

"I am. I have recently inherited from my father," I said, trying to remain calm. There was no reason for any of us to be frightened.

The man handed me a piece of paper, and I scanned it. They were conducting searches of all the nearby houses.

As if I couldn't read, one of them spoke up. "We are searching all the houses surrounding the inn. We are confident nothing is in your house, but the man punished today might have hidden objects in your other buildings."

He didn't seem to believe he wouldn't find anything. To me, it looked like he thought we were all guilty, but I supposed that was his job.

"You won't blame us if you find things we don't know about, will you?" I asked, worried.

"Of course not. We know what types of devices he carried. None of the people here would have access to such things."

They pushed past us and began to investigate the upper floor. It took them nearly an hour to search the entire house and associated buildings. During that time, no one went to work. We all remained silent and frozen, waiting for them to finish and for our farm to be declared clean.

"Get everyone lined up in the yard," the first man said to me when they had finished their investigation.

"Why?" I asked. He gave me a dark look. "I mean, why, sir?"

"We need to search your people, too."

I didn't like this, but I instructed everyone to assemble. Annalee stayed by my side. She looked sick from fright, and I knew it was because she had recently seen a man killed. It was enough to make any of us afraid. For someone coming from another planet, it must be unimaginable.

First Sun was high in the sky, making us all hot, with Second Sun about to rise. Third Sun was still on the other side of the planet, chasing his brothers across the sky in an endless circle.

I was surprised when the second man knelt at Mrs. Boyko's feet and picked up her skirt.

"Hey," she said, kicking at him.

"My companion will check your skirt hem for anything illegal, ma'am."

He felt around her entire hem and moved on to the next person, who was a man. He was forced to empty all his pockets as the Bureau man patted him down.

"People who have contraband often keep it on their person," the first man explained, walking up and down in front of us while the second man continued searching. "They are afraid we will discover things. They mistakenly think hiding them on their person is safer."

"Jesse," Annalee whispered into my ear. "I have to go to the bathroom."

"Right now, you can't," I hissed back.

"I have to." She seemed desperate, and I shrugged.

When she began walking away, the first man barked at her. "You there. Where are you going?"

"To the privy," she said, as quietly as possible.

"No one is allowed to leave until our search is complete."

"I really have to go," she insisted. "I'm at the end of the line. I'll return before you reach my spot."

"What if you are trying to get rid of illegal substances before we search you?" he said with a smug smile.

"Are you kidding?" she said. "I know how seriously this planet regards the law."

"Are you new to Yordbrook?"

"Yes," she said, choosing not to elaborate. She lifted her hands. "Okay, okay. I'll hold it. But I'm blaming you if I have an accident."

She seemed unconcerned and playful, but I knew she was lying. And the first Bureau man also realized something was wrong.

"Search her next," he said, flicking his head at Annalee.

Shit. She was standing beside me, looking calm and relaxed, but I could feel the tension coming from her body.

The second man knelt down at her hem. She gave me a glance that was meant to be reassuring but only amplified my concern. He felt around, and I held my breath. Did she have something in there? Was that why she was so nervous?

"I have something, sir."

My heart stopped. I looked at Annalee in fear. She didn't look like an innocent woman being unjustly condemned. She looked guilty.

His companion appeared immediately with a knife out. He cut along the hem and gently shook it. Something fell out into his hand.

It was a technological device. She had smuggled it in.

I glanced at her in consternation.

Why would she have done something like this? No wonder she had been afraid. Why hadn't she disposed of it while they were searching the house? Was she stupid?

And even before today, when she had seen a man killed, she could have destroyed the device or hidden it somewhere. Anything that would prevent it from being found in her possession.

The first man from the Bureau held up the device triumphantly. The yard was as silent as a funeral.

"This woman has been found in possession of technology. In two days, she will be executed in Willford with the other lawbreakers."

Annalee closed her eyes in pain.

They couldn't take her from me when I had just found her. I was starting to realize I cared about her. And now she was going to die.

111

CHAPTER 9

ANNALEE

Have you ever imagined what it would be like if people spoke the way movie trailers sound?

Dying was the easy part. Breaking my promise to Kyle? That was going to be hard.

None of it was true, but it sounded good, at least. I don't know what I was thinking, but part of me thought I would be above the law, or they wouldn't catch me with my phone. Maybe they would give me a special off-worlder's dispensation.

I didn't get any mercy, and now I was going to die. In retrospect, all of my decisions seemed bad. Coming to this planet, keeping the phone, marrying Jesse, and dragging him into this nonsense.

Becoming a teacher wasn't that important. I did good work with those three-year-olds. Kyle loved me...if he still remembered Miss Annalee. Maybe he had forgotten me by now, and I had risked my life to keep an empty promise to him.

Strangely, I didn't regret it, not even now in the middle of a disaster. I looked around and saw sympathy in some eyes but disgust in others. One thing I didn't see was a single face in the crowd that looked like they might help me. That included my new husband's. I stepped forward and held my hands out together, not looking at anyone and trying to be brave.

Someone spoke. "Sir, she's new to Yordbrook. She doesn't understand our ways." It was Mrs. Boyko. She was defending me, bless her heart.

"Ignorance of the law is no excuse," the Bureau man said curtly.

Before they pushed me into the cart, I heard Jesse's deep voice ring out across the yard.

"May I say good-bye?"

"Who is speaking?"

"I am," Jesse said calmly. "She's my wife."

"Be brief," the Bureau man said, stepping away to converse with his companion. I didn't turn to Jesse. Instead, I listened to his footsteps as he approached.

I thought about how he had made me feel last night and our aborted year together. I wasn't planning on staying longer than that.

When Jesse walked around and put his hand under my chin, making me lift my head and meet his eyes, I wondered if I might change my mind before the year was up.

He didn't hesitate but leaned in and kissed me slowly, deeply, as if he were learning my lips by heart and storing up the feeling to remember me by when I wouldn't be here anymore. It was hard to believe that he was the same grumpy man I married yesterday.

I lost myself in him as he wrapped his arms around me, pulling me tightly against him. As his lips brushed my ear, I heard him whisper only four words, but they gave me hope.

"Be ready. Don't sleep."

I held my breath as he stepped back. There wasn't an indication on his face that he had said anything to me.

"I will see you on the other side of death," he said, loudly enough for the crowd to hear. There was the sound of a woman's muffled sobbing.

He whispered, "It's something we say when we think we're seeing someone for the last time."

I nodded, unable to speak. Jesse backed away as one of the Bureau men came around and shoved me roughly into the cart.

"The execution will take place in two days." He smiled cruelly at Jesse. "You're welcome to come and watch her die. It serves you right for marrying an off-worlder."

I saw Jesse's lips tighten, but he didn't say anything. The Bureau terrified all the natives here. I didn't blame them. I was intimidated myself.

But Jesse had implied he would try to come and save me. I couldn't imagine Jesse the farmer rescuing me. Hadn't that been what he meant? I didn't know for certain, but I clung to the small hope and infinitesimal amount of comfort it gave me.

As my cart bumped and bounced down the road, I started to cry. How had I ended up here? Would my grand adventure end tragically? I would have to wait and see what kind of an alien I had married.

As if things weren't bad enough, now it was raining.

I still wore the long blue dress given to me when I arrived at the planet. It went all the way down to my toes and was long-sleeved, covering me completely. Right now, I was thankful it had a hood. I drew it to my face as the rain drizzled down on me. It had been pouring for hours. Pulling it closer didn't really made a difference. The water had soaked through my clothes, and I was shivering with cold, but doing something proactive made me feel better.

There weren't many things I could do to comfort myself. I wrapped my arms around my middle and huddled against the side of the cart, hoping the day would end peacefully with a washroom. I would kill for a chance to relieve myself.

The jolting of the cart had rattled my head all day long. I lost my glasses somewhere in the mud, and I wanted to get out and dry myself. I wasn't anxious to go to sleep. If I didn't escape or get busted out by someone, I would have the opportunity to sleep forever starting tomorrow. The thought gave me chills.

Abruptly the cart stopped. A Bureau man came down and unhitched the back of the wagon, pulling it out roughly.

"Get down," he said, jerking me off the back of the cart without warning. My legs had fallen asleep. They buckled under me, but I managed to stand my ground after a slight sway. I didn't want to collapse and show weakness in front of these men. "We're staying here tonight."

"I need to use the restroom," I said. "And change into dry clothes."

He snorted at the audacity of a woman asking for what she needed, but he reluctantly brought me to a small building on the side of the main one. It appeared we were at an inn, but a more desolate and less prosperous one than the inn near Jesse's home.

I went to the privy and discovered another problem. It was difficult to relieve myself when my hands tied in front of me. The guards refused to untie me when I went in, so I was forced to be creative, especially considering my dress and various layers of underclothes.

I managed to do my business and get my hands washed in the basin. I even managed to put all of my clothing back in its proper place and get back out without asking for help. My reward at the end was a stern-faced man shaking his head at me as I emerged.

I ignored him and followed in silence as he made his way around the puddles and moved toward the primary building of the inn. He brought me to a small room with no bed or furniture of any kind. It might have been a storage room before its present use as a cell. There were no windows.

116

It wasn't a modern jail cell, but I knew it would keep me confined as well as the highest security prison on Earth. I hesitated in the doorway. The Bureau man gave me a hard push. I fell, twisting to avoid landing on my hands and possibly breaking a bone. I didn't need to add that to my list of problems. Instead, I took a hard hit on my hip, and my head smashed into the floor.

I lay stunned for a moment before I could sit up. I held my head, trying to remove the dizziness. Once I felt well enough to stand, the door had been shut and locked for a long time.

There wasn't a way out of the small room. Aside from the door, there was no opening other than a vent, which was so high off the ground that I couldn't see where it went. The door was made of solid wood. I threw my body against it, trying to force it open, but I didn't weigh enough. It wasn't going anywhere, and picking the lock was beyond my abilities.

I felt like I should do something but there wasn't anything to do, so I sat down and waited. After a few minutes, I stood up and started to pace. The day stretched into the night and soon I was in total darkness.

I hadn't done much all day, but I felt dead on my feet. I hadn't gotten any sleep the night before. Jesse had kept me busy doing anything but sleeping. I didn't dare sleep now, though, since Jesse had told me to stay alert.

My eyelids were terribly heavy. To keep myself awake, I walked up and down in the room and talked to myself. I recited the multiplication tables. I sang every song I could remember. I tried to avoid certain thoughts. Things like Jesse never coming, and that if I fell asleep, I might never wake up.

I felt sick to my stomach without eating any food all day. Someone had put some water into my cell at some point during the day, but it was no substitute for the delicious bread they made here that's like nothing I had ever tasted on Earth.

I had eaten many loaves of it since my arrival on Yordbrook. Surprisingly, I hadn't gained a lot of weight, but Porter said they used a different type of grain for bread here. Apparently it both tasted great and had fewer calories.

Finally, I felt so tired that I leaned against the wall and tapped out a rhythm with my hand to keep myself awake. If I sat down, I would certainly fall asleep.

I tapped on the wall. *Tap, tap, tap-ta, tap-ta, tap.* Over and over, until a rustle inside the room made me stop.

What was that? Were there rats at this inn? On our way to Jesse's home, Porter had sometimes made us press on late into the night to reach the best inns. We often would pass by two or three because he said their service was subpar.

When I asked him about it, he explained he meant they watered down the wine, used the same sheets for multiple guests, and had cellars full of rats that ran wild through the building at night while the unsuspecting guests snored away.

This place had not looked prosperous, and I wouldn't be surprised if it were infested. The thought of being trapped in the dark with an unknown number of rats was as terrifying than anything I had encountered so far, including the thought of my death tomorrow. The rodents were with me right now.

I held my breath, listening attentively for another rustle or the feeling of something running over my shoe. It was hard to hear anything because blood was rushing through my ears. At least I no longer felt sleepy. Then I heard it.

Tap, tap, tap-ta, tap-ta, tap.

And again after a moment.

Tap, tap, tap-ta, tap-ta, tap.

It was the same rhythm I had been tapping on the wall. I froze for a moment, but when it came again, I was ready and tapped it back.

Someone was here. I hoped it was Jesse.

CHAPTER 10

JESSE

I didn't know if anyone occupied the house or not, but it was my best chance. It was where Porter usually stayed while in the area. I was sure he had a hangover, and he couldn't have gone far. Porter said he was leaving, but didn't go into specifics about where he was going. If he was still in the vicinity, there was a good chance he was staying here for the night.

I hoped he was there. I needed his help if I was going to save Annalee.

"Porter!" I yelled as loud as I could. "Open up!"

There was no answer or movement from inside. Nothing. If I couldn't find him, I would have to try and break Annalee out by myself. I had some skills, but I doubted I could do everything alone.

I heard a small sound and followed it around the house to a window. I peeked in and saw Porter and a beautiful young woman in the middle of a moment of passion.

Immediately I averted my eyes from the sight of their tangled bodies which were barely hidden by the sheets. I didn't need to see that. I couldn't hide from the sounds of their fucking. They were too loud to ignore as they both reached their climax at almost the same moment. It was impressive, even for Porter. It deserved applause.

I walked back around to the entrance. Porter had definitely not heard me yelling at him. After a few minutes, I began calling out to Porter again. I leaned against the door, waiting for something to happen.

Without warning, it opened, and I fell inside to see the lovely young girl standing in her shift. I shook my head. *Of course* the beautiful girl would be opening Porter's door for him. He was too lazy to do it himself.

"Where is he?" I said, dispensing with the pleasantries. I needed his help immediately. Night was falling, and Annalee's execution was in two days. The sooner we could get her out of the Bureau of Purity's grasp, the better. If they brought her to Willford, we would have to deal with heavy security. The best opportunity to free her was right now.

"He's not here."

"Yes," I said, interrupting her and staring her down. "He is."

Apparently my gaze was not intimidating this girl at all. She wasn't afraid of me. "He said to tell whoever it was to go away."

"The bastard," I muttered. The woman was shocked at my choice of language, but he knew my voice as well as his own. I was sure he could hear me yelling.

When I threw the door open, Porter was sitting up in bed, looking sour.

"I wanted to have her for the third time, Jesse. Couldn't you have waited a while? Or not shown up at all."

I didn't waste any words.

"Annalee's been taken by the Bureau of Purity. I need your help."

Porter sprang out of bed in an instant, holding the sheet up to cover himself.

"How did this happen?"

I shook my head. "She smuggled in some tech, Porter. I didn't know anything about it, and I couldn't do anything to help her."

"It's not a mistake?"

"I saw everything happen in front of my eyes," I said. All the ramifications of Annalee's actions suddenly struck me. Before I had only been concerned with the thought of losing Annalee. When I wanted to get Porter's help, I could only think about finding him. Now my mind had nothing to occupy itself. His question brought everything to the front of my brain.

I would be badly affected by all of this because she was my wife. Not only would I lose my Annalee, but I might also lose my home. Much depended on the Bureau of Purity investigation and whether they thought, as her husband, I had been helping her to conceal her items.

If I sat back silently and let her die, they would *probably* find me innocent because we had only been husband and wife for a short time. But that path would abandon Annalee.

On the flip side, *not* abandoning Annalee meant we would be assisting a criminal, someone charged with the worst crime imaginable on Yordbrook. Once we helped her, we would no longer be considered innocent in the eyes of the Bureau of Purity.

In fact, we would be on their shit list forever. We would have to go on the run or possibly leave the planet. As a side note, they would seize the farm.

All my dreams shattered in an instant. I felt a thick darkness come over me as I realized it was over. All the work...all the striving...everything my father wanted was now gone.

But my father would never let me abandon Annalee if I could prevent her death. I wouldn't let myself abandon her.

When I remembered her, I saw in my mind's eye how she looked when I made love to her this morning. I knew I had to see her again, even if it was only to chastise her for being foolish and risking her life.

"Jesse? You still there?" Porter said. He put his hand on my shoulder. "We'll get her back. Don't worry."

"Sure. Now that I know you'll help, I'm not worried about that anymore." I sighed. "This is really the end,

Porter. We have to turn our backs on our lives this time. There's no coming back."

He nodded, his face looking different without its usual cheerfulness.

"We knew it would come to this eventually. You can't do what we do and expect to live a normal life."

"No," I said, feeling sad. "I guess not. But that didn't stop me from hoping I could have everything."

"That's impossible. Everyone has to choose a side. It's time for you to decide." I stared at him, not wanting to admit that he was right. "Since you think Annalee is worth risking everything, it looks like you've made your decision already."

I nodded. And in my heart, I felt an ache as I let go of the dream of running my father's farm and turned my face toward an uncertain future.

"I have what we need," he said.

"We have to get her away from them before they get to the populated areas where they will have more assistance. Heaven help us if we have to deal with the security at Willford."

"That's right. We'll have the greatest chance of success if we grab her tonight."

A few minutes later, Porter was kissing his latest conquest goodbye. She stared at us as we strode into the gathering darkness.

We crawled through the bushes on our stomachs to avoid a guard standing watch outside the building. I assumed there was also someone on alert on the inside of the building, but I doubted they would be paying attention unless their partner sounded an alarm.

Although we had carefully wrapped the contents of Porter's backpack, it still made noise. Porter glanced at me and nodded at the guard. Now that we were closer, we could see their setup. Annalee was in a storeroom inside the inn. There was one guard outside and another man positioned in the building.

The exterior guard wielded a crossbow. The Bureau had a reputation for carefully training its men. We didn't want to get his attention. He could easily shoot both of us from this distance.

"Are you ready?" Porter whispered, making sure to avoid speaking too loudly. The wind was blowing in the guard's direction, and we weren't sure how easily they could hear our conversation.

We had already decided what to do. Porter wanted confirmation.

"We move ahead with the original plan," I said. "I'll meet you inside."

"Aye, aye, captain," he whispered. His words sounded brave, but I could see he was worried from his body language.

"What's on your mind, Porter," I said, putting my hand out to stop him before he crawled away. I needed him to focus on the task at hand, not distracted by random thoughts.

"Nothing," he said, looking away from me. I didn't say anything. "Okay, it's something. We've done this before, but it was never someone we cared about."

"We?" I asked wryly.

"She and I got to be friends while we traveled," he said innocently.

There was truth in his face, but there was something he wasn't saying. "I guess you've known her longer than I have," I said, hating that it was true.

He nodded. "It makes a difference," he said. "I don't want to screw this up."

"We haven't made a mistake so far," I said confidently. Internally, his nervousness was infecting me. If the Bureau agents guarding Annalee suspected we were trying to break her out, they would kill her immediately, and us soon after.

The Bureau was given a lot of flexibility when it came to dealing with enemies of the state. The law required them to give Annalee time before her execution, but there were ways around the minor technicalities. They could say she was resisting or attempting to escape when they shot her. No one would question their decisions.

I hoped we could get Annalee out. Porter and I had helped many people escape before, and we knew a bit about evading Bureau men. Porter had briefly worked for the Bureau of Purity. He knew how they thought and their protocols. It was useful knowledge in a situation like this.

We looked at each other briefly, then touched our fists to our foreheads. Porter held my gaze for a moment before he turned away and silently crawled off.

Unbidden, an image of Annalee came into my mind. She had kissed me tenderly in the moonlight as we lay close together and passed into slumber. I told myself I would get the opportunity to hold her like that again.

I wasn't sure how I had come to care about her so much in such a short time. I certainly didn't believe in love at first sight. It must be because I had married her. We took marriage very seriously on Yordbrook. There was no such thing as divorce here. When I made my vows, I meant them.

That was why I was here, right? To protect her?

I could almost convince myself that my only reason for being here was the vow.

I slowly counted to a hundred and finally set to work. I pulled a hollow reed from my pocket and placed a dart inside it. Porter and I had spent hours perfecting the art of hitting a target with this instrument. By this point, I could do it with my eyes closed. I crawled forward until I knew there was no way I could miss.

I knew I needed to hit him in the neck. I took a deep breath and let it out slowly, focusing on the spot I wanted the tiny dart to strike. The projectile went flying straight at the man.

He jumped and swatted at his neck, thinking that a bug bit him. Then he rubbed at the spot. He would experience minor pain similar to an insect sting. I couldn't see it from my location, but I was sure the projectile had fallen on the ground where no one would never find it.

He mindlessly massaged his neck some more, and I knew the dart had vanished, leaving no trace of what had knocked him out. A moment later, he slumped down and lay still in the grass. One down, one to go.

I went over to him and checked his pulse. It was regular, so he was still alive. As I was checking out the Bureau agent, I heard it.

Tap, tap, tap-ta, tap-ta, tap.

Was it Annalee?

I leaned over to the wall. *Tap, tap, tap-ta, tap-ta, tap.* I was excited to hear someone, hopefully, Annalee, tap it back to me again.

I crept inside and held still, listening for any noises. The biggest problem in old places like this was inadvertent creaks in the floors. I eased down the hall, creeping as slowly as I could and testing my weight before each step.

In this part of the hallway, a Bureau agent was guarding a prisoner. He was fast asleep, even snoring slightly. I felt cocky, but as it turned out, I was overconfident. When I took a step, the floor groaned and gave away my position.

The snoring stopped, and the guard's eyes opened. I retreated into the shadows, hoping he would not notice me. He looked for the source of the noise but didn't see me. I carefully prepared the blow tube, quietly lifting it to my lips. I got lucky. He started checking in the opposite direction. I had a chance if I moved before he turned around.

I stepped out, aimed, and blew. The dart hit the side of his neck as I stepped back. I was already hidden again when I heard his body fall to the floor. The drug-tipped dart would affect his short-term memory. When he woke up, he wouldn't remember a thing.

Porter appeared and helped me lift a heavy bar across the prisoner's door. When I pulled on the handle, it opened easily.

It was Annalee. My heart soared when I saw her, but not before I noticed her eyes light up with relief. She was glad to see me.

Reunions would have to wait until we were safely away. Porter had taken care of the other people who were awake at the inn to avoid witnesses. If anyone discovered us now, there would be a bounty on all our heads.

I dragged the guard inside the cell, dumped him on the ground, and barred the door again. We moved quickly out of the inn. Porter had tied up the other guard, who was still snoring soundly. I grabbed Annalee's hand, and we all ran quietly into the night.

Annalee wasn't in shape for an extended run. When we came to a clearing, Porter said we could take a break. I put my lips on hers immediately as she pressed herself against me. I let myself linger before we finally broke off the kiss, which was quickly becoming inappropriate for anywhere except the bedroom.

"You came to get me," she said.

"Didn't you think I would?"

She shrugged, looking uncomfortable. "I didn't know. Nobody in the crowd seemed like they would help me, including you."

"Plenty of us would help you if we could. I had the opportunity, so here we are."

"What do we do now?"

"I hope we get the chance to lay low and sneak out of here." I trailed off, looking around as my ears heard something coming from the woods. "Be quiet," I said, forcing her to crouch.

We hid behind some bushes and watched someone come into the clearing. Another Bureau man. They had an endless supply of these guys. I didn't know where he came from, and it didn't matter. Perhaps he had arrived to help the men escort Annalee to the capital. The only thing that mattered was evading him.

He would spot us sooner or later. We needed the element of surprise.

"It's time to go," I whispered, taking her hand. I jumped up, pulling her with me and we ran into the forest.

A voice rang out after us. "Stop. All of you are under arrest. If you continue resisting, I will shoot to kill."

I spotted Porter running ahead of us. I knew he had something that would help us escape. He would come back and get us when he retrieved it. Annalee and I took a different direction to confuse our pursuer.

"You're going to have to run. Pull your skirts up to your hips." She was struggling with her dress.

She didn't answer me, but I saw her pull her skirts up, exposing her shapely legs. She ran for all she was worth. We came to a stream and jumped over it, never slowing for an instant.

The Bureau agent behind us had stopped shouting. We could hear his feet pounding behind us. His body crashed through the underbrush. Porter was nowhere in sight. We kept moving as quickly as we could, but I could tell that Annalee was lagging. It must be harder for a woman to run with all the clothing. I pulled her into a zig-zag pattern to make it more difficult for anyone to catch up with us.

I knew she wouldn't make it much longer.

Finally, I saw something over the treetops. It was the glint of moonlight on a type of metal that had not come from Yordbrook. I knew it was tracking us, so I pulled Annalee under cover, trying to conceal us.

The machine overhead disappeared, and I cursed internally, not wanting to waste any more breath on speech. Annalee had started holding her side. She was bent over and starting to stagger. I felt myself beginning to slow down.

He was going to catch us.

I looked back over my shoulder but couldn't see him. Had he lost our trail or taken a wrong turn?

Because I was looking behind me, I wasn't paying much attention as we burst out of the forest and into a small clearing. Unable to stop my momentum, I smashed straight into the hull of a sleek, shiny state-of-the-art hovercraft, like few people on Yordbrook had ever seen. Annalee gasped and looked around, thinking she might be executed merely for seeing the object.

When it finally opened for us, Annalee didn't move. I roughly pulled her inside with me. As the door closed, she turned to me.

"What the fuck is going on here, Jesse? And who's piloting this thing?" I could tell she had a suspicion.

The man at the helm was busy cloaking our vehicle and maneuvering it off the ground. He answered Annalee without looking up.

"It's me," Porter said, his fingers flying across the console. "And now that we've left the Bureau below us, we need to get the hell out of here."

Annalee looked at me and started tearing off her dress.

"What are you doing? I'm sure you're glad to see me, but this certainly isn't the proper time."

"Don't start," she said, unbuttoning her dress as fast as she could but studiously avoiding a glance in my direction. "Don't act like you care about me."

"Of course I care about you," I said. I didn't understand why she was upset and struggled to control the anger rising inside me. "I risked my life for you and abandoned my life-long dream of inheriting my father's farm."

She stopped undressing for a moment. "I'm sorry," she said. Emotionlessly, she added, "Thank you, Jesse. The problem is that you let me think you were just as traditional as everyone else on Yordbrook. Apparently you two have no issues using modern technology." Annalee's face looked thoughtful. "In fact, if I had to guess now, I'd say you were part of the Underground."

It had felt wrong to deceive her, but I didn't have a choice. I couldn't have told her about my involvement before now. Many lives depended on compartmentalizing knowledge about the Underground.

"It's more than that," Porter said when I didn't answer immediately. "We're part of the Underground's leadership."

CHAPTER 11

JESSE

Annalee continued to disrobe. Layer after layer disappeared until she was standing in her shift, giving me an erection and making me move slightly to conceal my hard cock.

"Why are you undressing?" I asked, moving uncomfortably as my pants became cramped. "I appreciate the view, of course, but we're not a clothing-optional planet."

"Is this hovercraft fitted up to Union standards?" she said, looking irritated.

"Yes."

"Where's the bedroom?"

I motioned to the far end of the ship, and she vanished. I wondered if she wanted me to follow her into the bedroom. But considering the look on her face, romance seemed the last thing on her mind. I thought it was safer to remain I was. Porter had taken us high into the air and was flying at a reckless speed. He was trying to get us to headquarters as quickly as possible.

When Annalee returned, she looked quite different. She was wearing a pair of blue standard issue pants and a T-shirt. I had only seen clothing like that when I had left the planet on Underground business.

The pants fit her perfectly. They had a mechanism inside that sized itself to the wearer. The T-shirt showed off her fabulous breasts. It was tight against her body, and I wondered if she had done it to tease me. If she had, she would pay tonight when we were alone in my quarters.

"I am sick of those dresses," she said with vehemence. "Has anyone here ever thought a woman might want to get out of a carriage by herself?"

Porter and I glanced at each other.

"Are you trying to go back to the dark ages or something?"

I looked down at the floor and then back up at her face, thinking about how I could best answer to her question.

"Technology almost destroyed us once. We don't want that to happen again, and we're not sure what to do," I murmured.

"People almost destroyed your civilization," she said. "I hope you're not hoping you can save your people with restrictive clothing because it's not going to help." Annalee walked up beside Porter where he was resting. The ship was on autopilot.

"How are you, Annalee? You're looking beautiful in your non-restrictive clothing," Porter said.

"I've been better. The two people I've trusted the most on this planet have been lying to me."

"Jesse swore an oath, Ann. He's a good man. The best," he said, meeting my eyes and then looking back at Annalee. "He's saved my butt more times than I can count."

"We've saved each other," I said. "Now can you stop talking about me like I'm not here?"

She looked over at me. "Explain yourself, then," she said, her tone demanding as she crossed her arms over her perfect breasts.

"When Porter and I were younger, we found a computer."

"The one that got you the tattoo?" she asked. "Porter was with you at the time?"

"That's the one," I said "Porter was smart. He poked at it but said we should leave it where it was. I couldn't resist."

I looked her carefully in the eyes. "I took it home. It still worked. I was fascinated by the beautiful photographs and what it could do. For three wonderful weeks, I kept it under the floorboards in my room and learned how to use it when I had spare time. I hardly slept. My family was starting to wonder what was going on."

Annalee glanced at Porter, who was staring into space. He knew what came next.

"Then they found it."

"Who?"

"The Bureau of Purity. It was a standard search. They conduct them regularly."

"That sounds impossible. How could they find it? Surely they wouldn't look under all the floorboards in every house?"

I shook my head. "No. That's where their hypocrisy comes in, Annalee. The Bureau of Purity uses technology to find contraband technology."

"What?" she said, in outrage. "Are you fucking kidding me?"

I winced. I still wasn't used to hearing profanity in a woman.

"Sorry," she said. "Are you kidding me?"

"He's right," Porter interjected. "I worked for the Bureau for three years. When I left, I had a high clearance level. I learned about the types of technology they use. They don't hesitate to eliminate anyone if they suspect you'll reveal their secrets."

"How did someone that's part of the Underground end up working for the Bureau?" Annalee asked.

"That's coming later," I said. "They found the computer in my room, and I'm sure my guilty face told them everything they needed to know."

"You didn't look guilty at all. You looked angry that someone had taken your toy away."

I laughed. "A little of both, I suppose. A year later, someone approached me in the woods and offered to teach me some secrets if I joined the Underground. At that point, I understood the risks more clearly."

"It took him nearly half a decade before he finally gave in," Porter said. "I'd been working for them for a couple of years before he relented."

"How did you end up with the Bureau?"

"I went undercover. I learned a lot of information and somehow escaped with my life. I keep under the radar now and live in the shadows. If they find me, they're not going to do anything nice to me."

Annalee looked horrified.

"That's why you hid when the Bureau showed up at the inn. I thought you were a coward."

"The laws here are no joking matter, Annalee." I stood and walked over to her. I took her hands and gazed into her eyes, hoping she could understand. "I trust you realize how close you came to death."

"I know," she whispered, her face white.

"I'm not sure you do. It was reckless of you to bring a phone here in the first place. Once you saw the man killed, why would you keep it?"

"I..." She turned away. "You'll probably think it's silly. But I made a promise to a child to keep his picture with me wherever I went. It was stupid, I guess."

"You can call it silly, or stupid, or whatever," I said gently. "If it happens again, we might not be able to rescue you."

"I'm sorry. I never thought my actions would affect someone else. Does this mean they're coming after you too?"

I nodded. I wasn't sorry for myself, but I felt sad for my father.

"I am a horrible person," she said, sitting down in the co-pilot's seat. "I always thought I was a good daughter, but the truth is I resented my mother and how she wasted our money."

Her eyes filled with tears. "Now I've taken away the only thing you ever wanted."

She put her hands over her face, silently sobbing.

I looked at Porter helplessly. "Annalee, I never would have been good at farm life. I belong with the Underground. You helped me realize it. I would do it all over again if I had to."

"You said that you and Porter can't take any more missions like this."

I put my hand on her cheek. "I meant we didn't like worrying about the prisoner. We've never had to break out someone who was important to us. All our rescue missions had been for strangers before."

"Oh," she whispered. "You two care about me?" She looked back and forth between us and dropped her head, looking bashful.

"Porter's your friend," I said. "I am another friend and your husband. Of course we care about you."

She nodded silently, seemingly overcome by her emotions.

Porter coughed. "Anyway," I said, returning to the original topic of conversation. "I joined the Underground, and I've been working for them since then. I don't advertise the fact, of course. I somehow believed that I could do both forever. I was a fool."

"It's all my fault," Annalee began, looking anguished again.

"No, Annalee. A man must choose his side. He can't straddle two worlds. He has to make a decision and stick with it. It was time for me to choose..."

"But..."

I continued if she hadn't spoken, making sure to meet her eyes. "...and I have."

Porter looked up as the monitor began to flash.

"We'll be landing soon," he said, turning in his chair and tapping at the console.

"Where are we going?" Annalee asked.

I gazed out the window down into the forest. Even though I couldn't see anything yet, I knew the place like the back of my hand. I would know it in my sleep.

"The Underground headquarters."

ANNALEE

"Just give me a minute," I said.

Jesse seemed like he wanted to fix something between us, but eventually, he nodded his head and let me go. I wanted to be alone right now. I made my way to the bedroom where I found my new clothes and flopped back on the bed, staring up at the ceiling.

What I learned in the past half hour left my head spinning. I tried to list everything out so I could make sense of things.

First of all, Jesse and Porter had risked their lives to get me out of the clutches of the Bureau of Purity men.

Second, to do that meant Jesse was giving up everything he and his father wanted. Surprisingly, he didn't seem too upset. I guess Jesse meant what he said: it was time for him to choose a side. He couldn't be a traditionalist by day and part of the Underground by night, like a Yordbrook Batman. I imagined the double life was tearing him apart.

Third, we were all on the run now, including me. I had inadvertently broken the law on this planet. Being a criminal wasn't something I had intentionally done before. It would make it harder to get off-planet when it was time. Maybe the Underground could help. I wondered if they had ships taking off and landing on a semi-regular basis.

Fourth, I wondered what was going to happen when we arrived. The two men certainly seemed excited to get there.

I stopped listing things when I started thinking about how comfortable and practical pants are. There was a gentle bump and the sound of the hovercraft powering down.

We had arrived.

As I stepped out of the hovercraft (without any man's help, I might add), I drew in a sharp gasp. Everything looked normal here. Outside was a large hanger. After only a few steps, we arrived at something that appeared to be the main control room.

The enormous space was curved, and there were screens on all the wall. The displays showed various places on Yordbrook. One screen focused on the space station that was the main way on or off-planet.

People stood in the middle of the room. They worked on consoles floating around them, speaking into the air.

"Okay, stop right now," I said, and both Porter and Jesse turned surprised faces my way. "How in the name of all that's holy does this planet have any level of modern technology?"

JESSE

It was better to tell her everything now, so she knew the entire story of my planet. I had given her a shock earlier, and seeing her look of betrayal hurt my soul. I didn't want to keep any secrets from her.

No one had approached us yet. I led her to an unoccupied bench. We sat down together.

"Remember one thing about us," I said. "Our planet is not a Phase 1 world. We are no longer a developing civilization. We are a Phase 3 world that chooses not to use technology that we once had."

Annalee nodded silently.

"In the beginning was The Before Times. We call the time after the bombs The Between Times. We rarely mention The Between Times. What happened then doesn't fit well with our current version of history."

Porter spoke up. "An interim government arose during The Between Times. There was a dramatic decrease in population, but the people who survived wanted to get their old lives back."

"There was a problem," I said, reclaiming the narrative. "The biggest challenge facing the government was whether we should return to the old ways that led to the destruction or choose a new path. A few people wanted to go back to The Before Times. But a majority thought that was a mistake, and voted to adopt a simpler way of life."

"That's how Yordbrook ended up this way?" Annalee asked.

"Yes," Porter said. "Ever since those times, there has always been a minority who believed we made the wrong decision. When we constructed the official government and passed laws restricting technology, the Underground was born as well."

"We are merely the current leaders. One day, we hope for an open-minded regent who will grant us an audience and begin negotiations with the Underground."

"Wow," Annalee said.

"There are rumors that our planet's leaders want to reintroduce technology, but the timing has never been correct. Since we don't have an inside source, we think they're fantasies," Porter said with a shrug.

"These headquarters are hundreds of years old and were built right after the bombing. We kept the hovercraft running. They are all vintage, perfectly maintained ships from The Before Times," I said, looking around as I spoke.

"With state-of-the-art modern cloaking technology, of course," Porter added.

"I can't believe it," Annalee said.

"It's true." I was looking for Sheera. I found her barking orders at someone. The three of us and our fourth partner, Dayne, were the Underground leadership.

ANNALEE

My mind reeled as I contemplated the backward history of Yordbrook. Meanwhile, an excited hum buzzed through the room. A pants-wearing woman came over to us.

"Jesse," she said. "Porter. Welcome back. I see you've brought someone with you."

"I'm coming back to stay, Sheera."

Her eyebrows lifted. "Are you, now?"

"We had to extract Annalee from the Bureau. They'll be looking for me when they realize I disappeared the same day they lost my wife."

"Wife?" she asked.

"We were recently married."

She looked at me. "You're not from around here, are you sweetie?" The endearment grated on my ears.

"How did you guess?"

"You wear those pants like you were born in them. Most Yordbrook women come to like them eventually, but if this were your first encounter with them, you'd look a lot more uncomfortable."

"Sheera," Jesse said, trying to take control of the situation again. "This is Annalee, my wife. Annalee, this is Sheera,

147

one of the other Underground leaders. She's in charge of Headquarters."

"Nice to meet you," I said, holding out my hand to shake.

Sheera looked surprised. "You really aren't from Yordbrook, are you?" she asked, taking my hand and shaking firmly. "It will be fun to have another modern woman around here."

Her face looked pleased, but I was getting a strange vibe from her.

"We've had only a little sleep," Jesse said. "We're all exhausted, Sheera. I think we'll head over to our quarters now. We can debrief in the morning."

"I'm happy to see you again and to meet you, Annalee."

I nodded and smiled blankly. At the mention of bed, I realized I could barely hold myself up. I tried not show it, but suddenly keeping myself upright was taking all my strength.

Porter was only a few doors away from us. We said goodnight and retired to our rooms.

"I've missed showers," I said as Jesse closed the door. Sweat drenched my clothes. The temperature in here was much higher than outside. He opened another small door that opened into a private bathroom.

"Here you go."

"Is this bathroom just for us?"

148

"Yes."

"We have a toilet and a shower and everything?"

"You'll find soap, shampoo and anything else you might need."

"I feel like I've died and gone to heaven," I said.

Jesse grinned. "Not yet. But you will once I get you in my bed," he said. I narrowed my eyes.

"If you think I'm doing anything else except having a shower, you are gravely mistaken," I said. No one was getting between me and that shower, not even the sexy man in front of me. "I need to sleep, and so do you."

"Oh no. Take your shower and get nice and clean. I have plans for us."

My skin heated at the thought. I knew I was blushing.

"You do?"

I shivered and hurried into the bathroom.

"No need to dress when you come out," he called from the other room. "You won't need any clothes."

CHAPTER 12

JESSE

All I had wanted was to lose myself in Annalee's body. We lay in each other's arms. I watched her breathing softly. We had made love and fallen into a deep sleep. I had just woken up, and I wasn't sure what time it was. I thought it might be early morning.

"Jesse?" Annalee asked, sounding drowsy but happy.

"Yes?" I smoothed her hair back from her forehead.

"Why doesn't the Underground set up a way for those who want technology to leave the planet? Why do you bother fighting the Bureau of Purity?"

I sighed. "It's complicated, Annalee."

"Explain it to me. I want to understand," she said, lifting her head.

"The Underground isn't interested in getting into a war with the Bureau. We want to reintroduce technology in a controlled manner that's safe and makes life comfortable for everyone."

"What do you mean?"

"We don't want to change things and make Yordbrook into a modern planet. But we don't want our best and our brightest leaving Yordbrook to use the Internet, either."

"Don't you think once you open the dam, even slightly, all the water will come rushing out?"

I laughed. "We hope not. We believe we can bring back technology in a way that makes it invisible. If we keep it hidden, the beauty of our planet won't be disturbed. A slow introduction will let us evaluate everything and decide if we want to incorporate it into our lives. We're not going to have a war again."

"That sounds idealistic."

"Technology nearly ended our race. The Underground hasn't forgotten it even though traditionalists think we have. We have no desire to repeat the sins of the past. With strict rules in place, Yordbrook will never have that kind of violence or devastation again."

"Oh," she murmured.

"We hope to gain the convenience of technology. We know it can break down barriers, provides education, and connect us to each other. The trick will be avoiding the bad things that come with it. In time, an elected council can make decisions, and the burden won't be on the monarch alone."

"You're pretty passionate about this."

"Yes," I said. "I suppose I am. I believe in the Underground. We will be successful in reintroducing modern inventions in a way traditionalists can accept."

We were interrupted by banging on the door.

"Jesse!" It was Porter. "Get your ass out of bed. The Bureau has captured Dayne."

"Who's Dayne?"

I didn't answer Annalee right away, but got up and started putting on my clothes. Since Annalee was only wearing pants and a T-shirt, it took moments to make us presentable again. I opened the door and Porter stormed into the room.

"Annalee, Dayne is another Underground leader. Where was she taken, Porter? What happened?"

"I'll explain as we go. She happened to be in the wrong place at the wrong time," Porter said. We headed for the main control room with Annalee marching behind us. "The Bureau of Purity is doing simultaneous raids all over the world. It's a new tactic, and it's useful to them. There was nowhere to run. They attacked all our safe houses at once."

"How could they locate all our locations?"

"We think there must be a traitor among us. There's no way they know every place we're hiding."

"Have Sheera begin questioning everyone."

Porter nodded. "You'll need to take over Dayne's area as well as yours."

"Why me?"

"You have the least responsibilities right now, Jesse. You've been undercover. One of her advisors will brief you on what's been going on."

"Who's getting her out?" I asked.

"Sheera is putting a team together as we speak."

When we arrived at the control room, it was a mess. Everyone was talking at once. We were trying to communicate to everyone that our safe houses weren't secure, but it was a difficult thing to explain. Every minute was crucial.

Sheera came to us immediately. "Have you heard the news?"

"We heard," I said. "We need to start questioning everyone."

She looked at me strangely. "The king is dying."

Porter and I froze. "Are you sure?" Porter asked. He had always been sick, but it seemed like he would live forever.

"Our source at the palace says the doctor has given him only hours to live."

"Maybe this is our chance," I whispered, looking back and forth between my old friends.

"Maybe," Sheera said grimly. "But if he dies and we get the chance to negotiate with the new monarch, we need to be ready — and preferably not with our organization in shambles."

153

"Exactly," Porter said. "We need to find the traitor. I'm going to run scans on all the equipment used in Dayne's area. I might be able to trace the security breach to a particular device. Then we can figure out who used it."

"Was she wearing her locator patch? We should be able to correlate the position of the device and the location of the agent to identify our suspect," Sheera said.

"I'll get on it." Porter reached for a console that was floating near his head.

"Can I help?" Annalee asked. We had forgotten she was there. Porter and Sheera looked at me.

"I'm not sure," I said. "We can try to find something for you to do. In the meantime, why don't you get some rest?"

I was trying to be kind. I could tell she wasn't interpreting my response as kindness. She looked dead tired. I knew Sheera, Porter, and I would be busy for hours. At the same time, I knew she wanted to be useful.

She nodded and started walking away, but not before I saw the hurt look in her eyes.

"Annalee, wait," I said, catching up to her and touching her shoulder. "I'm not going to give you a mindless task so that you can feel better."

"Of course not," she said, with tears in her eyes. "I don't know everything that's happening here, but as an off-worlder, there should be something I can do."

"When we think of how you can help out, you'll be the first to know." She nodded, rubbing at her nose. I kissed her forehead.

"Sleep. You won't be any good to the Underground if you're too tired to see straight."

"That's true." I hoped she was feeling better. "Thanks, Jesse."

I watched her walk away until she was out of sight. I had to figure out a way to protect Annalee, discover her potential, and fulfill my responsibilities to the underground.

Sheera cocked her head at me. "That's something new."

"What?"

"I haven't seen you worry about people's feelings or be considerate before."

"I've been known to be thoughtful from time to time," I said, mildly annoyed with my old friend. I hadn't liked her treatment of Annalee. Sheera was one of my oldest friends in the Underground, and she always acted like an older sister.

"You could have fooled me."

ANNALEE

I was confused and tired. I was also having culture shock again, having learned about a hidden civilization on Yordbrook that wasn't in the travel brochures.

I made my way back to our quarters and lay down on the bed without changing my clothes. I didn't think I'd be able to sleep. I couldn't stop thinking about Jesse and Sheera. Had he slept with her? Jesse hadn't shown any reaction to her, but it seemed like he had some history.

Jesse and I had almost nothing. No history and barely a friendship. We were good in bed. But two people who go home from a bar for a one-night stand could be good in bed together. There was nothing unusual about that. I felt ill, and I slowly recognized the emotion simmering in my body.

It was jealousy.

I felt mildly disgusted with myself. How low-class! My mother was the kind of woman who would be jealous of someone working with her man. I certainly didn't want to be anything like my mother.

Jesse was my husband, and he had promised to protect me and honor me. I had to believe he would keep that pledge.

I must have drifted off into an angry nap because an explosion woke me up. I jumped up and ran out of the room. There was chaos everywhere. People burst out of their rooms, and everyone was talking at once. The lights in the hall weren't working. I felt my way along a wall, trying to remember the way to the control room.

By the time I arrived, there was light, but there wasn't anything I wanted to see. The members of the Underground fought with men in navy clothing — the Bureau of Purity had found them. There was an enormous hole in the wall where a bomb had gone off. I didn't want to enter the scrum because I wasn't particularly skilled at fighting.

I tried to find Jesse and finally spotted him in the corner of the room. He and Porter were fighting back-to-back as if they had done this many times before.

I was about to try and escape on my own when I felt a cold blade at my throat.

"What have we here?" I couldn't see the man's face, but I recognized his harsh voice. It was same nameless Bureau agent who had captured me back at the inn. I didn't say anything, but I wanted to cry out for help. My heart was pounding in my chest. I wondered if Jesse would assist me again.

As soon as the thought crossed my mind, I got mad at myself. What kind of a modern woman would expect her husband to save her?

"Come with me," he said, putting additional pressure on the blade. I slowly moved with him out of the room. He led us down the hall and took a turn I hadn't used since I arrived. As I moved further away from everyone else, I became frightened, and my imagination took off.

What was he going to do to me? If he was going to kill me, why didn't he do it right away? Where was he taking me?

We emerged in a garage full of personal hovercraft and boarded one. By this time, I had an idea of what he wanted. Once we were on the ship, he finally took the knife away from my neck. The Bureau agent forced me into the rear of the vessel where there were no doors. He moved into the pilot's chair.

"Where are we going?"

He looked at me emotionlessly. I squirmed in my seat. He was making me more uncomfortable than before.

"We've learned more information about you, Mrs. Melnyk. We didn't know the full extent of your husband's criminal activity. He's more than another Renegade."

Shit. He knew Jesse was one of the Underground's leaders.

"You will make fine bait," he muttered to himself.

"You can't use me to trap Jesse. I won't let you."

"I don't think you can stop me. And once we've caught you and your infamous husband..."

He became immersed with pre-flight procedures and didn't finish his sentence. I had to know what he was going to say.

"Once you've caught us?" I said. "Then what?"

"With the Underground fractured, there's no way for them to regroup without their leaders. We're going to make a public example of both of you to discourage others."

"What kind of an example?" I asked.

"We're going to kill you."

CHAPTER 13

JESSE

I slammed my fist into a man's skull, and he fell to the floor. Unconscious or dead, I didn't care. Porter smashed into me when his head was rocked back by a particularly brutal punch from a Bureau man. Porter came under his guard and delivered two blows to his guts, bending him over. After he had kneed him, the Bureau agent fell to the ground.

The brawl was coming to an end, and it didn't look like our side had won. I could see some of our people on the ground. Others had been dragged off by the Bureau.

"It's time to get out of here, Porter," I said. "Through the back. Annalee's in my quarters."

"Are you crazy?" He glanced across the room to the door that led to housing. If we wanted to get to the bedroom, we would have to get past a bunch of Bureau agents.

"You're right, Porter. You can escape and save yourself. Help me if Annalee and I get caught."

He rolled his eyes. "As if I'd leave you with this lot by yourself," he said.

We took off running and screaming at the top of our lungs, looking like madmen. The Bureau men were slow to react. We manage to barrel through three of them, but the next one knocked Porter on his ass.

Porter was up again in an instant. We took his assailant down together, kicking him a couple of times to make sure he didn't get back up. The next thing I knew, something hit me on the back of my head, and I fell flat on the ground. I blacked out for a moment. When I managed to get on my feet, Porter was in trouble. I jumped on the back of the man opposite him, giving Porter the edge he needed to finish him off.

By now, the way to the bedroom was clear. We took off running out of the control room. I was glad Annalee had been safe when the trouble broke out. If she kept the door closed, she wouldn't have even heard any noise.

I visualized what would happen in my mind. I could get her, grab a hovercraft, and hide out somewhere, as long as it wasn't a safe house. If we were able to lie low until everything blew over, we would be secure. Raids weren't anything new to the Underground. We couldn't lose the opportunity to present our agenda do the new monarch and the new government.

Porter reached the door first and knocked loudly, then threw it open when he didn't get a response. She wasn't in the room.

"Maybe she's in the bathroom," I said, opening the door. I looked around the small, empty room in dismay.

"Where is she?" Porter asked. I knew he suspected the worst because I did too.

"I don't know. She's not here."

There was a commotion in the hallway. The Bureau was beginning a systematic search of the area.

"We have to go, Jesse. We can't let them catch us."

I nodded. It would be the end of the Underground if they caught all the leaders. We left, quietly making our way to the garage. It was quiet and dark; apparently the Bureau had left this part of the facility untouched.

As we sped off into the early morning light, I wondered where Annalee was and if she was okay.

"There must be some way to track her," I said. I was finding it hard to think correctly.

"You know the Underground exists for a reason, right? It's going to be difficult to find her without any advanced technology. I don't suppose you happened to put a GPS patch on her?" Porter said.

I shook my head. "If I stored things like that at home, the Bureau would have taken me prisoner along with her. I didn't think it was necessary."

"Our options are limited, then. We don't have enough manpower to search all Yordbrook on foot."

"There are only a couple of possibilities, though. The Bureau could have captured her again, or she might have escaped with one of our agents. Either way, we should be able to track her easily. It rained recently, and they probably left a trail."

"That's right," Porter agreed. "If she's with one of our people, they headed for the rendezvous point, and we'll find her there, assuming the Bureau doesn't know about it already. If the Bureau captured her, then they'll take Annalee to Willford."

Neither one of us wanted to guess if Annalee was alive or dead.

"Sounds like we have a plan. Let's find some people to help us look for her."

By nightfall, we had been unsuccessful. We had found some other members of the Underground who escaped, but she wasn't anywhere in a five-mile radius. I didn't want to give up the search, but Porter made me face reality. The Bureau had captured her.

We had no choice but to go to Willford. Further searching on foot wasn't going to help. We returned to the hovercraft and Porter set the course.

"Why do you think they would take Annalee instead of killing her outright? They knew she was a wanted woman."

"It's likely they circulated her picture as soon as she escaped. Every man ought to have recognized her. There's only one reason I can think of," he said.

"They're going to use her against me, aren't they?"

"I think they'll use her to lure you in so they can capture you, and then they'll kill you both and make an example of you. We still don't know where Sheera is either, in case you've forgotten." Porter sighed. "What are we going to do?"

"The same thing we always do - figure things out as we go along," I said, laughing at him. "Don't worry. Annalee is strong."

I thought she was strong, but internally I was worried myself. We were going into enemy territory with nothing but our wits.

ANNALEE

My guard pushed me roughly into the prison cell. I had spent so much time in Bureau captivity on Yordbrook it seemed like my second home. I stumbled and fell, hitting my head on the corner of a desk in the room.

"Fuck," I said. I put my hand on my head and felt a trickle of blood running down my face. The guard barely acknowledged my injury as he shut the door.

I held my hand to my head in an attempt to stop the bleeding. I now had a pounding headache to go along with my sore cheek. My legs started to feel weak, so I sat down on the single chair in the room and surveyed my surroundings.

The cell was small, cold, and dark. The only illumination came from a high window. It was more like a hole in the wall; it looked barely big enough for my arm to fit through. On the bed was a narrow cot with a wool mattress, like the ones at Jesse's house. A worn but clean sheet and a threadbare blanket completed the furnishings.

I hoped they treated their prisoners well here. I wasn't sure where I was, but by eavesdropping on the conversations around me, I thought they had moved me to Bureau Headquarters. I didn't know why they bothered. I was just a random off-worlder. Why were they making such a big deal about me?

They were keeping me alive as bait in a Jesse trap. But they didn't need to bring me here like I was someone important. My hands were free, at least. I slipped off my shoes and sat down to rest.

I had only been left alone for a minute before the door violently opened, and a blonde woman wearing a bright red dress walked in. Her scarlet hood framed the pale white skin of her beautiful face and made her look terrifying. Her eyes were light blue, like chips of ice.

She looked at me disdainfully.

"Get her some proper clothes," she commanded, and walked out again. After a few minutes, another Bureau employee appeared in my cell and threw clothes for me on the floor.

I waited until he was gone, then picked them up. I sighed, thinking about all the bits and pieces I would be required to wear again. I looked forlornly at my jeans and T-shirt as I pulled them off and started the laborious task of getting dressed in a beige dress and hood.

Fortunately, it didn't take me as long as I had imagined. I guess I was getting better at dressing myself. I refused to put on my shoes, which didn't fit properly and hurt my feet. I didn't bother with the socks either. The small act of rebellion made me feel better. Soon the door opened again, and the woman returned.

She held her hands behind her back and began to pace around the room in front of me. The woman was young. She wore a plain navy dress that stretched to her toes and a matching hood that covered her hair. Although we wore similar clothes, she had an aura about her that reminded me of an army commander.

"Mrs. Melnyk." For a moment, I wondered who she meant. I slowly realized she was addressing me. It was the first time someone called me by my married name, and it felt strange.

"I have paid careful attention to your stay on Yordbrook. You've done many things in a short period. You started as a simple case of an ignorant off-worlder in flagrant violation of our laws, then became the bride of an Underground leader, and now you're a prisoner of the Bureau of Purity once again."

"Who are you?" I asked. For some reason, the names of the Bureau agents who kept capturing me were unimportant, but I wanted to know who this person was.

"I am the head of the Bureau of Purity. You may refer to me as Controller Kozel."

"How can you be the head if you're a woman?"

She glared at me.

"I thought women played a subordinate role in Yordbrook society."

"That might be true for some jobs, but it's certainly not the rule for the entire planet. I am the fourth female Controller, so there is a precedent. After The Before Times, we thought having women in positions of power would give us a more balanced perspective."

"Hm," I said, surprised. Obviously, I had more to learn about the people of Yordbrook.

"I am here to inform you of your pending execution. It will occur immediately before the new queen's ascension to the throne."

Apparently I wouldn't have much time to learn. "I thought you had a king?"

"We expect the king to pass away within the next few hours. People are already beginning to prepare for the new queen's coronation. The queen and the Bureau want to start off her new reign on the right foot, so to speak. If we execute you before the coronation, we will discourage any 'revolutionaries' from interfering with the Bureau of Purity.

An idea occurred to me. "Is it possible to exile me?" I said. I felt ill again at the thought of my beheading. I didn't have anything to lose if I asked for leniency. "As you said, I'm an off-worlder. I was ignorant of your laws."

"Ignorance is no excuse," she said coldly. I knew then that my fate was sealed.

"Why is the Controller of the Bureau of Purity coming to tell me about my execution? Are you trying to rub it in my face? I already knew that already. Anyone could have reminded me."

She pressed her lips together. I sensed she was angry about something but was trying to control it.

"I wanted to see what the wife of an Underground leader looked like before she died and I lost the opportunity. After our latest raids on the Underground, it will be extinguished in a matter of days. It's a glorious time for Yordbrook."

"We barely know each other," I said. When I looked at her carefully, she seemed to be fuming. She looked at me with contempt and hatred, but I hadn't done anything to engender such feelings.

I decided to go for broke. I was already going scheduled for execution. What else could happen to me?

"You're lying," I said, standing and looking at her in the eyes. "Why are you really here?"

A question from me was all it took to remove her veneer of civility. All her anger was apparent now, and she made no further attempt to hide it. When she finally answered me, it was through clenched teeth.

"Mr. Melnyk has had a string of women since he was a teenager. I was interested to know who the woman was that finally caught him."

With how many women had Jesse been intimate? Was she another one of his conquests?

The Controller looked me over with contempt. "You're not much to look at, are you?"

People were certainly superficial on this planet. Why was everyone here always commenting on my looks? I wasn't a hag or horribly disfigured. I was an average girl, pretty on a good day. I was getting sick of every alien I met telling me I was ugly.

I moved forward into her personal space and looked directly into her face. "I may not be much to look at, but Jesse married me. It seems like he prefers me to the others." I glared at her. "Does that upset you, Controller?"

"Nothing you could say could upset me," she murmured. "Jordan!"

The Bureau man who brought my clothes stepped into the doorway. This one had a name!

"Yes, ma'am?"

"Take the prisoner to the cellar for the night. You can return her immediately before her appointment tomorrow."

Jordan hesitated. "Are you sure, ma'am? There were no orders to torture her. Does she have valuable information?"

I blanched and started to sweat. Did he say torture? I had stepped over the line with someone who had complete control over me. Sometimes my mouth said things I regretted, and this was a perfect example.

"I've changed my mind, Jordan." She turned to me with a wicked smile on her face. "It seems Mrs. Melnyk needs to be taken down a peg or two. This way, she will be properly broken when she appears before the people tomorrow."

He made one more attempt to help me. "But ma'am..." She cut Jordan off with a sharp hand gesture.

"Move the prisoner. Don't question me again." She walked out of the cell without another look.

"Yes, ma'am, right away," Jordan said to Controller Kozel's disappearing back.

I stepped back until my knees hit the bed and I collapsed.

"There's no point in resisting, Mrs. Melnyk." Jordan looked apologetic. "It will only make things worse."

He bound my hands together and grabbed my arm, leading me out the door.

CHAPTER 14

ANNALEE

I stubbed my toes on the stone floor as the guard dragged me behind him. I tried to keep up the pace, but I fell a couple of times during the long trip to the cellar.

I regretted my prior decision to show defiance. I needed those shoes. Even socks would have helped protect my feet.

When he opened a door that led into black darkness, I finally put up some resistance and stopped moving.

"What's the problem?" he asked gruffly.

"I'm not going down there."

"Of course you are," he said, his eyes gleaming in the darkness. "This is the only way to the dungeons. You should not have antagonized the Controller. Now, instead of spending your last night in a comfortable, clean bed, you are going to spend it screaming."

He lifted me up and carried me through the portal against my will. On the other side, he put me on the ground again and we descended into the blackness. I stumbled on the stairs only one time, but it was frightening enough to make me be wary.

"Do these stairs ever stop?"

"We're almost there."

In the end, we came out into a broad stone corridor. Flickering torches at intervals in the wall provided light. The area smelled like shit and dirty human. I gagged.

"Sometimes the terror makes them lose control of their bowels."

I stopped and stared at the guard, who pulled on my bound hands again. "This way."

We came to a wooden door at the end of the long hallway. The guard opened it and gently pushed me in. I, of course, tripped over my feet and crashed on the floor. My face smashed onto the ground. I couldn't stop myself because my hands were tied. I blinked away the tears and sat up. My vision was slightly blurred.

Why couldn't they let me walk through the door like a normal person? I sensed I was about to get more bruises on my body. It didn't matter much if I was going to die in a few hours.

"What are you going to do to me?"

I had meant for it to be a harsh demand but it came out as more of a squeak.

He didn't answer me. He moved to a counter that stood against the wall. My eyes followed his movement and lingered on the counter. Sharp objects covered it. I wasn't interested in learning their purpose.

When the guard started walking toward me, he held a whip.

"You don't have to do this," I said, fear filling my heart. "Please, don't."

"I have orders directly from the Controller." He didn't look me in the eyes. "You brought this on yourself."

I closed my eyes and broke into a cold sweat. He walked around me and moved to the counter, taking his time while choosing from a selection of knives. I wondered if I would be able to hold onto my dignity. What kind of a person was I? Would I scream, or cry, or beg?

He took the knife and carefully cut the back of my dress from neck to waist. He neatly separated the pieces flopping into my dress, exposing my naked back to the cold air.

I heard a clatter on the stone floor. When I turned my head, he had dropped the knife. I gulped. Would I get a reprieve?

I looked at the weapon on the ground and back to the torturer, in the most doe-eyed manner possible. He still refused to look at me as he unfurled the whip.

When I saw the whip uncurl, I realized that he couldn't hold the knife and the whip in the same hand. For a second, I thought he was helping me, or didn't want to hurt me. Those thoughts vanished from my mind when I heard the sharp crack of the whip. The next thing I knew, I felt a sting of leather against the tender skin of my back.

Someone screamed.

On Earth, I had never been physically hurt before. I made sure to avoid all the bad parts of town and rarely saw violence. No one had ever hit me, and I had never been in a fight. Before the whipping, the worst pain I ever had was when I broke my wrist.

The lashing on my back hurt more than breaking a bone.

I don't know how long he waited. Seconds? Minutes? The whip cracked again, on a fresh piece of skin lower on my back. I screamed again. Every stroke hit new nerves I didn't know existed. Tears began rolling down my cheeks, and I wondered how much more I could endure.

After the sixth lash, I sensed a pattern. He was counting to twelve between each swing. I wondered if he had a reason for it, then the whip came again and I couldn't think. I was close to passing out.

The guard put the whip down and left the room.

Without my permission, my mind conjured an image of Jesse, with his handsome smile. I imagined him leaning down to kiss me.

I cried for what might have been and for everything lost. I was going to die at first light or second light or first light of the second sun or whatever they called it here.

The guard never came back. My back hurt less now, but I think I was in shock. I went in and out of consciousness, only waking up when my body twisted in my sleep and hurt me enough to force me awake again.

The night seemed endless. Without anything else to do, I replayed significant moments of my life in my mind. I kept coming back to the ones involving Jesse. It was in the darkest moments that I had the shocking realization I loved Jesse.

I didn't know how such a thing had happened so quickly. I barely knew him. But I also knew I loved him, as surely as I knew my name. I longed for him to come and save me again. But I was afraid I would be his downfall.

They only wanted me for bait. I was waiting in a trap that would result in his death. If I saw him again, that would mean they caught him, and he was about to die.

And secretly, selfishly, I did long to see him again. I needed to get out of here and stay alive so I could see him again and confess my feelings.

I looked around. The knife lay tantalizingly close to me. I thought it might be close enough for me to grab. I stretched out my foot. It almost touched the blade but couldn't quite reach it. I strained against my bonds, feeling rope cut into my wrists, pushing my body and moving my leg as far as it could go.

My toe barely touched the knife. It was a good thing I had taken off my shoes in my cell, even though I had wished for them many times. I had stubbed my toes and cut my feet on the way down into the dungeon.

Unfortunately, the knife moved in the wrong direction. It spun slightly and went further away from my body. I let out a small moan. The sound of my voice made me sick to my stomach. If I couldn't find inner strength, I was going to die.

I would do whatever I needed to do. I took a deep breath and reached as far as I could, farther than before, feeling the rope bite into my wrists and my muscles stretch to their limit. My toe touched it, and I carefully pulled it back towards me within reach.

I wanted to jump up for joy, but ropes still bound me, and I wasn't free yet. I reached for the knife and tried to put it between my toes. It took many tries, but I finally picked it up. Now that I was an expert in foot-knife movement, I promptly dropped the blade when I tried to move it to my hand. I had to make three more attempts before I could lift my foot my foot high enough and simultaneously grab the handle with my fingers.

I held onto the knife carefully and began sawing at the rope. Eventually, I cut through the last strand, and one hand was free. In a moment, I had the other hand loose, and I headed for the door.

It was locked, of course.

"You won't get out that way," a voice croaked from a dark corner of the room.

I froze. The knife was still in my hand.

"Who's there?"

"Just Jemima. I'm nobody, really."

I grabbed a torch from its sconce on the wall and slowly approached the sound. When I got close enough to see who had spoken, I gasped.

The elderly woman was so skinny her face looked like a skull and her eyes bulged out. How had she survived here by herself? There was a spark of light in her dark green eyes.

"Jemima? I'm glad to meet you, but I have to get out of here. Can you help me?"

She nodded with a cunning smile.

"How can I escape if I can't get out the door?"

"I shan't tell you," she said. "The man went down to the river to bathe and said 'Help me! Help me!' to the pretty maid," she sang.

"I'll do whatever it takes."

"Will you give me your first-born child?" she cackled.

I was prepared to do *almost* whatever it took. Was she crazy?

"It was only a jest. I will tell you what I know. I will never escape from here, but there is a chance for you."

I waited patiently. It seemed unlikely Jemima would have any information that was helpful to me, but I had no other options.

"There is a door which leads into the adjoining cell from earlier times. Once, these cells were filled traitors, those who participated in the destruction of our world. The ones who had set off the bombs. Back in the day, I hear they were piled fifty to a cell. The door let air flow into this room so the prisoners wouldn't suffocate. The other cell has a window. Can you see it?"

She looked up at me and pointed to the window. I nodded.

"The current guards have forgotten what this place once was. You can reach the door, but I cannot. At the bottom is a small mouse hole. If you reach into the hole, you will find a key from long ago."

If I had to reach into a dark mouse hole and get a few bites, so be it.

"After you go through the door, open the window and pull yourself out. I'm not sure what lies beyond. From there, your fate is in your hands."

"Thank you." I reached up to touch the woman's shaky hand for a moment. "If there's anything I can do to get you out, I will help you."

She nodded, but I knew she didn't believe me. My wrists hurt badly from where the rope had cut through my skin. My head throbbed, and I hoped I had enough strength remaining.

I didn't hesitate at the mouse hole, shoving my hand in and moving my fingers around. I groped around for a moment and found a metal skeleton key, but no mice, thank goodness. It was a small blessing in the midst of chaos and horror.

I put the key in the lock and turned.

Nothing happened. It was stuck. Just my luck.

I turned it again. This time, I heard the soft screech of metal and the lock clicked. I pulled on the door handle, and it slowly moved as if no one had opened it for a long time. I grabbed a torch and brought it with me.

On the other side, I ran for the window and wrenched it open. I need both hands to pull me up, so I had to leave my only light source. Even though every part of my body was in pain, the adrenaline and fear gave me the strength to lift my body up and out of the window.

Once I was outside, I stayed in the shadow of the buildings and ran. I found a road. I didn't know where it went, but at least it wasn't here. If I got away, I planned to leave this planet and never come back.

Jesse was welcome to come with me, but I had no desire to live in a place where the authorities threw people into dungeons. I understood that I broke the law, but what they did to me was inhumane.

Following the road led me to sparse trees which grew into a forest. Walking became a burden. All I could think about was moving one foot after the other.

I was growing more tired with every step, but I wouldn't give in until I was free.

The night began to lighten in the morning sky. First Sun was about to break. I felt a strange feeling. Was someone watching me?

Suddenly a man jumped up from behind me and grabbed me from the rear, trapping my arms. His hand covered my mouth.

I couldn't believe they caught me again so quickly.

CHAPTER 15

JESSE

Porter lightly landed the ship so lightly that I hardly noticed. He touched it down in a forest behind the Bureau of Purity headquarters. He shut off the engine but left the cloak running.

The Underground rarely used hovercraft on Yordbrook, but when we did it was important to engage the cloaking device and keep the ship hidden. We didn't need the general public to panic because they thought aliens were invading them. It would take a big leap in logic to guess their people were flying an illegal vessel.

I took a quick look at myself in the mirror. I had changed into more practical clothes from the storage compartment. I was wearing a black T-shirt and black pants. They felt comfortable. I noticed I had a black eye and cut lip from the fights.

I laughed to myself. I looked rakish, like a bandit. It was a far cry from the responsible farmer I had been a short while ago. My current appearance was a closer match to how I thought about myself.

I had wanted to please my father, of course, and have security. A farm was the only way to guarantee freedom on Yordbrook. But the inheritance had never been about what I wanted, but what my father needed to make himself feel safe.

Porter was waiting for me in another room. "Are you ready to go?" I asked. I don't think Annalee has a lot of time to waste.

"Don't worry about her, Jesse. The Bureau treats its prisoners well. She'll have clean sheets and a private cell for her last night on the planet."

"I suppose you're right," I said, but I couldn't shake the feeling that she was in trouble. It was probably paranoia. "Better safe than sorry. Let's get moving."

Porter nodded and opened the door.

We sneaked through the woods until we reached the edge of the forest. Crouching down, we surveyed the compound. Porter pointed to a building that looked the same as all the other buildings.

"There," he said. "That's the wing where they keep the prisoners."

We needed to get this right. There wouldn't be any second chances tonight. By the moonlight, I estimated the night was half over. Annalee would die at the first light of Second Sun.

"I'll be back as soon as I can," Porter said.

"You mean, *I'll* be back as soon as *I* can. She's my wife."

"No, I don't. You're not going in there, Jesse. They want to catch *you*. That's why they took Annalee."

"Aren't you're one of the leaders, too? They would be happy to get either one of us."

"They won't be looking for me. Especially since they think I'm still a Bureau employee." He held up a purple stone which identified him as a Bureau worker.

The Bureau controlled the distribution of the stones. They were impossible to counterfeit. The only way to get one was to be a Bureau employee. They were a practical identifier of who was with the Bureau and who wasn't. If anyone captured them, they were instructed to destroy their stone.

Of course, Porter kept his stone when he left the Bureau and went into hiding. He started changing into a dark navy Bureau of Purity outfit. His clothes and stone would probably be enough to get him deep into the compound.

It wouldn't help if anyone examined the stone in detail and realized that it had been missing for years. But if it worked, I suspected he would be able to go places I wouldn't be able to reach by breaking in.

I frowned at him. "This wasn't the plan."

"I don't know what your plan was. It always was the plan for me," he said, shrugging. "I need to go, Jesse. Annalee doesn't have much time."

He turned and began to walk away.

"Porter. Be careful."

He nodded once before he disappeared, leaving me to wait alone in the dark.

"What do you mean, she wasn't there?" I asked, feeling an empty sensation in my gut.

"I got in without any problems and made it all the way to her cell. The guard in the hallway said she had been taken down to the cellar."

"The cellar?" A horrified expression appeared on my face.

"That's where they torture people."

"I know! You don't need to say it!"

"I went down and found the guard who was assigned to 'educate' her and talked to him."

"Did you 'educate' him back?"

"No, I needed the information, Jesse. He was in his room already. Apparently he thought she was going to pass out, so he gave her a break. He planned to return soon so I asked if I could talk to her. When I got there, she was gone."

"Where could she go? Did the guard know she escaped?"

Porter shook his head. "There wasn't any commotion while I was there."

"Do you think he helped her escape?"

"I don't know. Maybe. It didn't bother him when I told him the prisoner had escaped."

It didn't matter. What mattered was her current location.

"I think she would have headed for the forest. She wouldn't know where to go, but the trees would provide natural cover. I'm not sure how I missed her, though."

"Maybe she came out on the other side and hid among the trees across from you. If you looked the other way for only a moment, it would be enough for her to disappear into the trees."

I pulled out a pair of night vision goggles. The Underground advocated technology, but it still felt odd to me every time I used it. They would help me see in darkness and detect a person's body heat from a distance, making Annalee easier to spot than if I were looking for her with my naked eyes. I snapped them onto my face. In an instant, I could see as well as if it were daytime.

"You should prepare yourself, Jesse." Porter put his hand on my shoulder.

"For what?" I asked. I felt impatient and wanted to get going.

"She may not be the same person you married," he said. "You know what I mean?"

"It doesn't matter," I said. I tried not to think of the terrible images Porter had conjured. "Let's go."

It was slow. We moved back and forth in a coordinated pattern, making sure we didn't miss any section of the forest. When First dawn broke, we avoided looking at each other. The Bureau would be coming after her. If they didn't know she had escaped yet, they would soon, and there would be Bureau agents everywhere.

I didn't say anything to him but kept moving. We both knew there was nothing to say. If we didn't find her and vacate the area quickly, we would have to leave without her.

That's when I saw movement in my peripheral vision. I removed the goggles; I didn't need to rely on gadgets after all. The gray light of morning was bright enough for me to see without them. The movement was from a human form.

"Is it her?" Porter asked.

The woman was beaten almost beyond recognition. Her dress was torn and disheveled. Ann had been wearing pants and a T-shirt when she left. I couldn't see her face very well, but it wasn't Annalee.

I shook my head.

"No matter who she is, she must have escaped the Bureau. We have to help her, Jesse. We don't know if we can help Annalee, but we can help a person in front of us."

He looked at me and then quickly ran toward the woman. I didn't want to move. Grief filled me, and I thought helping this stranger would be like giving up on Annalee. He went behind her, covering her mouth so she wouldn't scream and give away our location.

I saw her jump at first, but her body fell limp in defeat. I sighed, walking towards them. He was right. At least we could help someone get away from the Bureau.

"Jesse, I've got bad news. You can't recognize your own wife. She's badly hurt." I broke into a run.

ANNALEE

I tried to scream but a hand covered over my mouth, muffling my cries. Someone's arm held me tightly, and I couldn't get away from it.

I wasn't going back there, no matter what. I struggled and moved my arms and legs in any direction. My captor adjusted his grip. I was able to move slightly, and I decided to take a chance. I wouldn't let the Bureau get me again.

Somehow I managed to stomp on his foot, and he cursed. Then I shoved my elbow into his stomach as hard as I could. I succeeded in making him bend over, but he didn't let go of me. I wriggled my arms furiously. I managed to get one of my arms free and I flailed around, managing to hit him in the head.

Success! He grunted and relaxed his hold on me. I slid out of his grasp and started moving away as quickly as possible. I never saw his face. I didn't want to.

"Wait." There was something vaguely familiar about his voice, but I couldn't tell what it was. I only knew I wanted to run.

I took off as fast as I could. I wasn't exhausted anymore. My fear gave me energy and speed. I heard the sound of someone crashing through the vegetation behind me. I did my best to lose him, but my best wasn't good enough. Not only was he fast, but I also suspected no one had recently beaten him.

My pursuer caught up with me and went for my legs, tackling me. I didn't have much energy remaining at this point, and I went down hard. It felt like I landed on all my wounds simultaneously. I cried out, but they wouldn't take me again. I crawled forward on my belly, kicking with my feet and trying to get him off me.

He wasn't willing to let me leave, of course. When he got up, he pulled me with him and twisted my arms behind my back, making me yell out again.

"No!" I screamed. Like he was going to listen to me. But strangely, he released one of my arms and turned me around to look at my face.

"Annalee?" he said. "Is that you? I can hardly recognize you."

"Porter?" I ripped my arm violently out of his grip. "Why are you attacking me?"

"We were looking for you. Hang on a second." He cried out for Jesse.

"Why were you chasing me down like I was an animal?" Now that the excitement was over, my body started to shake from all the adrenaline.

"I didn't know it was you," he said. In fact, when he looked at me, it seemed like he still wasn't sure who I was. He pulled out a knife and began gently cutting the ropes on my wrists, which were cutting into my skin. I winced, and his eyebrows drew together.

Jesse burst into the clearing. "What is it?" he said, looking at Porter. "What's wrong?"

"This is why you didn't recognize her." Porter directed his gaze toward me.

A shocked expression passed over Jesse's face. I realized I must look pretty hideous. I didn't have a mirror, but I moved my hand up to touch my face. There was a cut and swelling on my forehead, and I imagined there were bruises on my cheek. My wrists were rubbed raw by the rope. My dress flapped at the back, revealing welts. The rest of the garment had been torn to shreds when it caught on bushes during my flight.

When I realized everything that had happened to me, I started to feel light-headed. Jesse was by my side in an instant, catching me as I fell. I didn't black out because I felt the first rays of sunlight coming through the trees.

Shouting arose in the distance.

"We have to get back to the ship, Porter." Jesse stood up, still carrying me in his arms. He looked like he was ready to run all the way back with me as baggage.

"You're going to have to put her down. If we're all going to live, she needs to run."

Jesse gently set me on my feet again. I tried to concentrate, but the pain made it difficult. It was starting to come back as the adrenaline faded.

"Annalee, you heard us," Porter said. "You know what you need to do."

We started moving. I had a man on either side of me. Each held one of my hands and helped pull me along. It was hard for me to keep up but when I stumbled, they caught me and helped get me on my feet again.

I wasn't sure how long we ran. Eventually, Porter said, "We're almost there." It could have been a few minutes, or it could have been an eternity. My muscles had stiffened up long ago. It was hard for me to move at all, but somehow I was still going, with their assistance.

When we reached the ship, Porter entered the code for the door. It made a soft beep. I leaned heavily on Jesse, my legs feeling weak. I was ready to sit down.

The door didn't open.

"What's wrong?" Jesse asked.

Porter shrugged his shoulders and entered the code again. The door still didn't open. We heard the sounds of someone moving behind us in the forest.

I willed the door to open with my mind, but that didn't have any effect either.

"I'm sure I'm using the correct code. Let me try one more time."

"What if they're using a scrambler?" Jesse suggested.

Porter froze. "I think you're right."

"So we can't get in?" I asked.

"Not if the Bureau's locking us out." Jesse turned around to look at us and immediately dropped to the ground.

I looked at the new threat. A group of Bureau agents had emerged and surrounded us. They were all pointing crossbows directly at our heads.

"Surrender," a female voice called out. The Controller walked into the clearing. She wore forest-green pants and a matching T-shirt, showing off her gorgeous figure.

What a hypocrite. I remembered how she had been disgusted at my modern clothing and forced me to put on the dress I was currently wearing. Now I wondered if she had made me wear the clothes to slow me down if I tried to escape.

"Why should we?" Jesse said bitterly, looking at her with hatred in his eyes.

"You don't want to be late for your execution, do you?"

CHAPTER 16

JESSE

I didn't hate many people, preferring to save that emotion for the most deserving, but Gwynnara was one of them. The feeling was mutual.

Gwynnara flashed a cruel smile as she told me I was late for my execution. Sleeping with her had been a youthful indiscretion. You can't always foresee the consequences of your actions. If we hadn't banned technology on Yordbrook, I would use a time machine (if they existed) to go back and warn myself to stay away from the crazy. I had no idea she would become Controller and eventually threaten my wife and me.

At the time, I was a teenager, and she seemed like an innocent farm girl. She seduced me with a bottle of morelia in her hand. For about a year, we slept together whenever we could.

When I didn't propose marriage, she asked me herself. I turned her down. I didn't know who I wanted to marry back then, but I knew it wasn't Gwynnara. I had discovered something underneath the innocent persona she displayed to the world. An aspect of her personality was desperate, cruel, and ruthless.

I supposed those qualities had helped her become Controller. When I turned her down, she had raved and screamed, but it didn't stop me from leaving her. A few months later, she became ill and was bedridden. I didn't see her for nearly a year.

When she re-emerged, she wouldn't even look me in the eye when our paths crossed. I didn't understand what had changed in our relationship. Once she became Controller, it seemed as though she always had her eye on me. Her men always harassed me when no one was looking. I think she knew I was a part of the Underground, but she couldn't prove it.

"Take the girl," she said.

"She can't walk. You've beaten her within an inch of her life."

"Oh?" Gwynnara's eyebrows shot up in mock surprise. "Really?"

She snapped her fingers towards some of her guards. They came forward carrying a stretcher.

"We certainly can't have the prisoner unconscious at her execution."

"Let Porter go with her, at least," I begged. I knew she wouldn't let me free.

"Where is Porter?" She looked around. He was gone.

"Search the woods for him," she ordered our escort. "He can't have gone far."

In fact, he had to be quite close to us. The only way for him to vanish like that was if he dropped down and

195

rolled under the spaceship. The cloaking device would shield him as long as no one discovered the vessel.

Our guards split up. Two left the clearing to search for Porter. Two carried the stretcher and loaded Annalee onto it. The rest came for me. I stepped forward and held my hands in the air. I didn't want anyone coming closer to the ship.

"Let's get on with it, then. It's a good day to die," I said, trying to mask my fear.

Gwynnara rolled her eyes and motioned for the men with the stretcher to go ahead. She let them advance just far enough so I wouldn't be able to see or hear Annalee.

"Jesse will come with me," she told her men. "One of you walk behind us. Shoot him if he tries anything. It can be somewhere painful, but don't kill him. We need to show him off during the execution."

The last thing I wanted right now was a heart-to-heart conversation with Gwynnara. As the men moved off, I couldn't keep up the veneer of cheerfulness any longer, and I felt my frustration show on my face.

All my efforts to save the farm and planning with the Underground had been for nothing. The Underground was in ruins with the leadership captured, safe houses destroyed, and people scattered. I would never have a life with Annalee because we were both going to die.

"Fuck," I whispered, feeling a black ball of rage start forming in my gut.

Gwynnara looked at me thoughtfully. It felt like she was staring into my soul.

"Yes, you always did like to," she said.

I couldn't stop myself. "And you didn't?" I said, bitterness against her coming out of my mouth. "Are you honestly going to tell me you didn't enjoy it?"

"Maybe I did," she admitted. "But none of that matters now."

"Because you're going to kill me."

"You broke the law, and the penalty is death. I have nothing to do with it," she said coldly. She averted her gaze but not before I saw a glimmer of uncertainty in her eyes.

Was there a chance? "You have power, Gwynnara. You could spare us."

"Spare you?" she gasped, turning to look at me in disbelief. "Why would I do that? I've been waiting for this moment since you left me."

The uncertainty in her eyes was gone. In its place was hatred.

I had chosen the wrong words. I didn't know she wanted me to die.

"Gwynnara, what did I ever do to you? We had a good time together. You know a marriage between us would have ended in disappointment. Why do you hate me?"

197

She started walking even faster, making me work hard to keep up with her. She certainly kept herself in good shape. I wondered if she was going to answer when she suddenly spoke and broke the silence.

"Do you remember when I was sick for a long time?"

"Yes," I said patiently.

"Do you remember how long it was?"

"About a half a year or so."

"It was exactly six months," she said. She stopped and looked at me. Fire shot out of her eyes. "As soon as I started to show, my family locked me up."

I froze. "What do you mean?"

"You got me pregnant, Jesse. You weren't around any longer. I was left to deal with the consequences of our actions by myself."

"Wait a minute," I said. "Why didn't you tell me?"

"Why would I? Do you think you would have helped me? You had already declined my proposal. I wasn't going to have anyone marry me out of pity, not even you," she sneered.

"Gwynnara." I sighed

"Don't even start," she said, holding up her hand. She resumed walking, and I scrambled to catch up with her.

"What happened to the child?" I asked under my breath.

"Do you remember my younger brother?"

"He wasn't your brother, was he?"

"No, he wasn't. He grew up knowing me only as a sibling. But when he was nine, something happened." She fell silent and pressed her lips together.

"I remember," I said. "He died of the fever."

She nodded quietly, turning her head so I couldn't see her face.

"Gwynnara, I'm sorry. I wish you would have told me. Then you wouldn't have had to go through everything alone. I might have known my son."

She drew in a deep breath. "It doesn't matter now. I have a plan to get even for all the pain. You ruined my life, and now you're going to pay."

We had reached the courtyard. Annalee was already there, standing on her feet. There was a crowd speaking quietly and waiting for the execution. They were all dressed in their best. I wondered why they would dress up for an execution.

I remembered the new queen's coronation was happening later today. They were quite efficient for the masses, giving them two entertainments for the price of one.

It was a chilling thought.

ANNALEE

I stood up and got off the stretcher. There were a lot of people around me. Everyone wanted to witness my death, I supposed.

When Jesse came up beside me, I wondered what he had said to the Controller. She stormed past us looking angrier than she was before. The Bureau had increased security around us. There were four guards armed with swords within reach. Further back were some men wielding crossbows. We weren't going to run away to freedom.

"Annalee," Jesse murmured under his breath. I shifted my eyes to him without turning my head. "I don't have anything left in my bag of tricks."

I gave a slight nod.

"I wanted you to know something." He trailed off when someone started to beat a drum off to our left. "I care about you, and I wish we had more time together."

I wasn't sure what to say. My eyes started to tear up against my will. Suddenly, my mouth started moving. "I care about you too, Jesse. In fact..." I took a deep breath. "I think I love you. And even though I may die today, the last few weeks I have felt truly alive.

It seemed like everything around me went quiet. Jesse reached out and took my hand. No one said anything or shot us, so I guess they didn't care about what we did anymore. I knew there was no way out.

As the beating of the drum intensified, I felt a sword poke me in my side.

"It's time, my love," Jesse said, looking over at me. I got lost in his beautiful blue eyes one last time, then forced myself to turn my head away and start walking again.

JESSE

Annalee's confession of her feelings for me was a bright spot, but I wouldn't have long to enjoy it. My hands started to shake as we walked toward two blocks of wood. The blocks of wood were for us to rest our heads on while the executioners swung their weapons.

They wore black hoods and held sharp axes. The blades could sever a head from its body in one blow if the man were skillful enough. I hoped these men were well-trained. I had no desire to wallow in pain while they swung their weapons two or three times.

The constant drumbeat made an already tense situation worse for me. The atmosphere was already morbid; I didn't need my final moments accompanied by a death march. We walked as slowly as possible, staying side-by-side. My throat tightened as I imagined that we might have faced many challenges at each other's side if given the opportunity.

I thought the blocks of wood would be disgusting and bloodstained, but as we got closer, I saw they were spotless. It looked like they had refreshed the wood for each of us. I wondered if it was a courtesy extended to everyone or only high profile prisoners.

The guards maneuvered us until we were kneeling and facing the crowd of people. Gwynnara began to speak.

"We are gathered here together today to expunge from our planet those might destroy it. We protect our people from corrupt elements who selfishly desire to bring down

Armageddon upon us once again. Today is a reminder that we are here to keep our children and our children's children safe."

She certainly had a knack for words.

Despite the gravity of the situation, Annalee snorted slightly and looked like she was fighting back a smile. If we were going to die, we might as well have a good attitude about it, I supposed. The knowledge of our powerlessness was surprisingly freeing.

"Technology destroyed our civilization once. We won't let it happen again."

A voice rang out through the courtyard. It was louder and stronger than Gwynnara's. It came from the person next to me. "Technology didn't destroy your civilization," Annalee said. "People did."

It was like something had sucked the sound away from us. People didn't talk and didn't move. We all knew the truth, but none was brave enough to say it. Annalee was calm and confident. She had nothing to lose.

"What does an *off-worlder* like you know about our planet?" Gwynnara said. She was furious that Ann was stealing the spotlight.

"I don't know everything about your people or Yordbrook," she said. "But I do know one thing. A tool is a tool, whether it's made from steel..."

She nodded her head at the axe beside her.

"...or circuitry. Why don't you make it illegal to own a knife or crossbow? If a person wants to hurt someone else, they could use one of those tools as easily as an advanced weapon."

The crowd murmured its assent.

"Enough of this nonsense," Gwynnara shouted, sensing she was losing control of the situation.

But Annalee wasn't done yet, and the executioners made no move to stop her.

"You think you're high and mighty. Everyone else in the galaxy is wrong. But you're trying to forget your history. Your ancestors thought it would be a good idea to press a button and end millions of lives in seconds." She paused. "That's what you're all afraid of, isn't it? You don't want to repeat the sins of the past."

"I said that's enough," Gwynnara repeated.

"Hiding from technology won't save you from yourselves," she said, looking around at the crowd that was staring at her in consternation. "You can destroy yourselves again with primitive weapons as well as with bombs. You're different people than your forefathers. The question you should be asking yourselves is, 'Have I learned anything from their mistakes?'"

She looked around and tried to make eye contact with anyone in the crowd that was brave enough to look her in the eyes.

"Your beliefs will save you. Nothing else."

Gwynnara moved to take matters into her own hands. She stepped forward and pushed our heads down onto the blocks.

"On my mark," she said. The executioners nodded.

"Say goodbye, Jesse," Gwynnara muttered under her breath.

"Now," she whispered.

The executioners lifted their axes overhead. I closed my eyes.

CHAPTER 17

JESSE

As Gwynnara gave the signal for the executioners to swing, I closed my eyes. I braced myself and prepared to see my relatives.

I imagined the executioners swinging their axes in perfect synchronicity. I wondered if they practiced their motions together.

I was going to die.

I waited for the horrible moment when the axe hit my neck, but it never came.

Instead, I heard the sound of metal against metal. My eyes flew open. My executioner had turned his weapon and blocked Annalee's executioner from cutting off her head.

What was going on?

I supposed Gwynnara was wondering that as well. She stormed over to the executioners.

"What are you doing?" she hissed. "You only have one assignment." She was furious.

"I know," said the executioner, pulling off his hood. "But it's hard to kill your best friend."

Gwynnara's jaw dropped. Annalee and I lifted our heads. "Porter," she muttered. "What are you doing here? Do you honestly think you can save them? Look around you, man."

She gestured broadly at the crowd.

"There's no one here who will help you," she said coldly. "You are all on your last breath."

She made a beckoning motion to the guards that stood along the sides of the courtyard. "Get another block. We are going to have a rare triple execution today."

"Porter," I whispered. "Now all of us are going to die. What were you thinking?"

"You worry too much, Jesse." Porter obediently held out his hands and allowed them to be tied.

When Gwynnara returned, she indicated an area to place a third wooden block. They roughly shoved Porter down and pressed his head into the wood. I could see Annalee's hands tremble, and I wanted to comfort her. There would be no comfort for any of us until we arrived on the other side of death.

Gwynnara was making another speech about the foolishness of going against the Bureau, but I wasn't listening anymore. I could barely concentrate. It seemed like I was living in a dream. We were going to die in minutes, and there wasn't a way out. Without Porter, there was no one to help us.

"We are going to try this one more time," said Gwynnara. "And this time, there will be nothing stopping us."

The executioners raised their axes again. Once more, I held my breath and closed my eyes, waiting for death.

But I guess it wasn't our time to die. The swing of the steel blades was halted again, this time with a shout from the Queen's Advisor.

"Halt," he commanded, running up breathlessly. "I order you to stop this execution."

"By whose authority?" asked Gwynnara. "No one who can stay the Controller's order."

"No one?" said the man. "Surely there is one person who outranks you, Gwynnara.

Suddenly the Controller looked less sure of herself.

The Advisor lifted his voice and spoke to the crowd and guards. "By order of the Queen, stop this execution."

"What does the Queen care about the Bureau's business?"

"There is a new monarch, Controller," said the man. His eyes were like steel. "She has different concerns than the previous regime."

Gwynnara typically had the authority to do whatever she wanted. The Advisor was showing her a different world, one in which she had considerably less control. As she stood open-mouthed, he began to bark out new orders.

"Bring in the prisoners," he commanded. His voice rang out in the silent courtyard. The guards looked at the Controller uncertainly. She had her fists clenched together but nodded her assent.

"Porter, how did you magically appear behind me?" I asked.

"I used the Bureau stone. And I called in a favor from a friend."

I wondered what kind of friend had that amount of power.

As the guards lead us away, the Queen's Advisor turned to the crowd again.

"There is a new ruler on the throne," he said. "We must be prepared for change."

His words seemed almost prophetic.

I certainly hoped things were going to be different.

It didn't seem possible that Annalee and I had escaped our sentence twice. I supposed we still had work to do in this life.

ANNALEE

I had been contemplating the role I played getting myself into this mess. I came to the conclusion that the situation I found myself in was my fault. Jesse hadn't thought anything like this would happen when we got married. He thought I was a sweet Earth girl who could help him keep his family farm. In fact, we had helped each other.

The Earth girl had gotten herself arrested and made him risk his life rescuing her. When I disobeyed him again, I got myself caught a second time. Eventually, we were caught and almost killed, only being spared by a miracle.

It was all too much for my conscience. I wanted to give Jesse a way to exit this relationship gracefully. I would tell him I planned to leave and return to Earth. I was sure he could find a more suitable bride from Yordbrook. Perhaps someone existed in the Underground who would understand him and not care about his tattoo. He would be better off if I got out of his hair.

I would give up on the money. I would lose it because I hadn't stayed married to him for a year. I would have to give up my dream of becoming a teacher, which was my reason for starting this ridiculous adventure.

Surprisingly, realizing that I would never be a teacher didn't bother me that much. Doing the right thing was more important to me than clinging to a dream. I had made some stupid and selfish decisions, but there was a way to fix everything.

What truly hurt was the realization that I would be leaving Jesse and never see him again.

"Please sit here while I let the Queen know her visitors have arrived."

Jesse looked at Porter, who shrugged, appearing as mystified as we were. I found it difficult to believe myself. A few minutes ago we were prisoners, but our status had quickly upgraded to visitors.

I hoped the Queen would be lenient on Jesse. Of course, it was foolish. He was an Underground leader; she was compelled to be harsh and set an example.

But there was a small hope in my heart, just the same.

We waited in silence. I wasn't sure what to expect in an audience with the Queen, but I was so happy to be alive I didn't care.

Jesse and Porter both looked awful. Even if they had been wearing their best clothes, they had dark circles under their eyes. And they weren't wearing their best clothes. Their attire was torn and dirty.

When Porter and Jesse first met me, I had looked horrible. I hadn't had the opportunity to fix myself. Now I was going to meet the Queen. I didn't think of myself as a vain person, but I wanted to look my best for royalty.

There was a floor to ceiling window down the hall. If I stood at the correct angle in front of it, I would be able to see my reflection. I dragged my tired body up to make myself presentable.

There wasn't much I could do about the bruises and bumps on my face, but I drew my hood up. It would cover my matted hair. Was that the only thing I could do? I had torn my clothing in many places. My bare feet were crusty with dried blood.

I returned to the men. "I can't see your Queen looking like this," I murmured.

"Annalee," Jesse said. "I wish we could attend to your wounds immediately, but the Queen is requesting our presence. She stopped our execution. I'm sure she understands that we don't look our best. It will be only a few more minutes."

"I get it. I don't mind going to see her. In fact, it's an honor." To be honest, I wouldn't have minded lying down and taking a little nap first. "The problem is that I think my appearance will be offensive to her."

"I find that unlikely."

"Perhaps I misspoke. Pitiful is more like it. What I meant was, she won't want to look at a wreck like me."

"I have heard good things about the new Queen," Jesse said. "I'm sure she will overlook your appearance, Annalee."

I nodded. I supposed I could try to hold it together and not remember that I looked like a hovercraft had hit me several times and landed on me. I would not think about the fact that every inch of my body ached. I would conveniently forget I could barely keep my eyes open.

I could be dignified and channel my inner strength. I would have to be myself, I supposed. I didn't have the strength to put on any masks right now.

The Queen's Advisor opened the door. "Would you all please follow me? The Queen would like to speak with you."

JESSE

We were lead into a small chamber decorated as a sitting room. We approached the Queen with our heads down. Annalee attempted a Yordbrook curtsy to the best of her ability. Porter and I bowed.

Annalee didn't fall over, so I considered the curtsy a success. When I looked up, I froze. I recognized the Queen immediately. From the shocked expression on her face, I assumed she remembered me as well. Her expression changed quickly, and I wondered if I had imagined the moment of recognition.

"Your majesty." Porter took her hand and kissed it. She looked like she was trying very hard not to react but her cheeks betrayed her. They turned pink. They were as bright red as they had been when I had inadvertently spotted her making love with Porter. The last time I had seen this woman was on the day I had gone to find Porter and ask him to help me rescue Annalee.

Porter's face looked like he was a man in love. How was Porter in love with and having intimate relations with our new Queen without me knowing anything about it? I glanced at him out of the corner of my eye, but he had no answers on his face.

I would have to get the whole story out of him after we left this room. If we had managed to escape death, we would be in a cell together for a long time, and he would have the rest of our lifetimes to tell me his tale.

"I wish to speak with the three of you," the Queen said.

We sat silent and listened. She was a beautiful young woman, with pale skin and elaborately braided brown hair. Her eyes were brilliant green, and her movements were graceful.

"I am young and new to the throne, but I have some ideas that I would like to discuss with others who may share my views."

Her eyes flicked briefly to Porter. He tried to hide his smile, but couldn't quite manage it. The Queen was doing a better job of remaining composed.

"Could you be more explicit about your views, your Majesty?" I asked.

"I understand my Bureau has arrested the men because you are leaders of the Underground."

"That's correct." There was no reason to lie.

"Mrs. Melnyk has been arrested for the crime of possessing technology she brought from another planet."

"That's right," Annalee said. She sensed the undercurrent flowing between the Queen and Porter, but couldn't understand it.

"What exactly do you want from us, your Majesty?" Porter asked. He gazed at her intensely. I doubted he was only talking about the present circumstances. Porter was thinking about his future as well.

The Queen lifted her chin and met the gaze of each of us before she spoke.

"I wish to open a discussion between the throne and the Underground."

"To what end?"

"I want to reintroduce technology to Yordbrook, Mr. Melnyk."

CHAPTER 18

ANNALEE

I felt like the Queen had just told me I could have my phone back. Maybe she had. "Excuse me, your Majesty. Did I hear you correctly? Do you want to reintroduce science to the planet?

The Queen looked at me. "Just because a person grows up on Yordbrook does not mean they are unaware of technology and its benefits. One of my uncles was part of the Underground."

"I was unaware of the Queen's position," Porter said, flabbergasted. He walked over to the Queen and took one of her hands. "You never told me," he whispered, staring into her eyes.

"It was never the right moment, and it would have compromised both of our positions."

Jesse and I looked at each other. We suddenly felt out of place, and I would have done anything to be allowed to slink quietly out of the room. Unfortunately, it looked like the Queen had many things she wanted to discuss with us.

"Did you know I was working for the Underground?" Porter asked.

"My family has been preparing me to become Queen for many years. We know everything that happens on Yordbrook, Porter."

Porter released her hand and ran it through his hair as he paced back and forth across the room. "When I asked for help, I thought you would arrange a diversion, not stop the execution."

"You needed my help, and I provided it. There is a new regime now, and change is coming."

Jesse seized the opportunity to take a step forward. "Your Majesty, could you explain your plan to us and how we can assist you?"

"Certainly, Mr. Melnyk. I'm sorry. I'm becoming distracted." She looked away from Porter and her cheeks turned a lovely shade of pink. "For many years, the rulers of Yordbrook have sought a solution to the dilemma our ancestors created on our planet."

"Dilemma?" I asked.

"Yes," she said, nodding. "That is the correct word. We face a dilemma. First, we destroyed ourselves using science and technology. Our response was to move in the opposite direction and declare technology evil. The truth was that we had destroyed ourselves. We were afraid we were going to do it again, and we overreacted."

"All this time, there were people in the government that wanted to bring technology back?"

"The stories were true," Porter mumbled.

"Yes," said the Queen. "But we could never figure out how to do it safely. Once the Underground increased its activity, we saw the opportunity. There was a grass-roots movement to bring science back. If we had issued a royal command, we would have had a revolution against the crown. This way, the idea comes from the people."

"I'm still shocked you knew about my role in the Underground and you never told me," said Porter.

"Porter," she said sharply. "We can discuss this later."

"Yes, of course, your Majesty."

Her eyes looked at him fondly before she turned back to Jesse and continued their conversation.

"The Underground has surreptitiously brought technology back to Yordbrook already. The challenge facing us is how to integrate it into our society, and convince our people that it is benign, not malevolent."

Jesse shook his head. "That will not be easy, your Majesty," he said sadly. "From birth, we are taught to abhor technology without questioning why. It will be a monumental task to overcome generations of education."

"I know," she admitted. "That's why the throne cannot do it alone. We need your help." She looked at each of us in turn. "Even yours, Mrs. Melnyk."

"Why would you need my help?" I asked. I wondered how I could be of use to the Queen.

"You come from a land where there is minimal fighting, but you manage to use science without destroying yourselves."

"I guess I do."

"We want technology without destruction. We hope you can give us guidance."

Without thinking about the audience in front of me, I plainly spoke my mind. "If you want peace, you should get rid of the Bureau." I said, gesturing angrily at my battered body. "And the torture chamber."

The Queen winced. "That will be one of the first orders of business," she said. "We apologize for our overenthusiastic agents." She came next to me and took one of my hands. She was careful to avoid touching my raw wrist where a rope had dug into the skin.

"I am sorry," she whispered, looking into my eyes so I could see her sincerity. "If I knew what was happening, I would have never permitted it."

I nodded, unable to speak, my eyes full of tears.

"We will need the leaders of the Underground to spread the word to their people and be evangelists for technology and the throne," she said, turning to the men. "You have to go among the people and show them it is not dangerous. The crown will ensure there are strict laws regulating science so we will feel safe having technology on our planet again."

"This is an ambitious initial project, your Majesty," Jesse said.

"I am aware of that, Mr. Melnyk."

Jesse's face broke into a grin – the one I loved.

"Can I count on your support?"

"Of course you can," said Jesse. "This is the chance we've been waiting for — a royal edict. You offer more than we could have ever dreamed. The most we had hoped for before was to ask for an audience."

"The Underground will help you," said Porter earnestly.

"Thank you," said the Queen. She gave Porter a graceful curtsy. The Queen was beautiful, and the attention she paid to Porter made me slightly jealous.

She waved her hands at us, and it appeared our audience was over.

As we walked down the long, empty corridor, Jesse practically exploded. Apparently he had been waiting to ask Porter about his relationship with the Queen.

"Porter, was that the woman that I saw at your safe house?"

Jesse glared at him, and Porter had the decency to look sheepish.

"Yes, it was," Porter said. "I don't regret it. She wasn't a mistake."

221

"Porter," said Jesse with a groan. "You can't jerk this woman around like all the other ones. She's the Queen. If you mess this up, she'll put you in the dungeon, and not merely give you the evil eye every time you come to the inn like all the others."

"Jesse, you're my best friend," Porter said. "But right now you don't know what you're talking about. I've got the situation under control."

Jesse stared at him, dumbfounded. "You think you love her, don't you."

"I don't think I love her," Porter said, his face as serious as I had ever seen it. "I know I do."

Jesse laughed. "I don't believe it!" he shouted.

"You should take a look at yourself before you decide what other people can and can't do. You're just as head-over-heels for Annalee. I never thought that could happen."

Jesse looked at me intently. "I suppose you're right," he said, putting his arm around me. The air went out of my lungs. I felt like I could hardly breathe.

Did he love me?

"I guess we're both different men now," said Jesse, leaning in and giving me a kiss. His touch made me forget the previous evening, the pain in my body, and everything else in the entire world.

We hadn't gone far when Porter excused himself. He seemed preoccupied with something. The next thing I knew, the Queen's Advisor had overtaken Jesse and me.

"Mr. and Mrs. Melnyk," he said. "Please wait a moment. The Queen wanted to make sure Mrs. Melnyk is feeling well. She has instructed me to take you to the royal physician for evaluation."

It was hard to believe. A few hours ago, I was being tortured in a dungeon, and now I was about to be treated by a royal physician.

"Yes, of course," said Jesse.

I looked at him blankly and finally lost control. I collapsed. He stepped forward and caught me, breaking my fall as I plummeted to the ground. I could hear voices as I fell unconscious. They were talking about carrying me somewhere, but at that point, I didn't care.

When I woke up, I felt like I was a princess. I was in a clean bed with beautiful soft, white linen sheets and thick quilts with lots of pillows under my head. I was wearing a white nightgown. I felt human again!

Doctors had bandaged my wounds and wrapped strips of cloth around my wrists. I could feel an ointment on my face. I lay on my stomach with more salve on my back. It smelled clean and fresh, with a hint of spicy herbs. Everything still hurt, but not as much. Just being clean made me feel better too.

I heard Jesse's voice from the other side of the bed. "Are you awake?" I turned my head to look at him and smiled even though I could hardly keep my eyes open.

"I'm awake. Now that we're alone, there are things I want to tell you," I said. "But so much has happened I feel like I don't know where to begin."

"It's okay. You don't need to say anything if you're not ready. You need to rest."

I gazed at him. He was handsome. I wondered if he truly cared about me, an Earth girl everyone else on this planet kept referring to as plain. When I first arrived, he had almost been cruel to me. I thought he would be unkind or even hurt me. I now knew he would never harm a woman.

But I knew more about him now than I did in the beginning. He was looking out for me, and I had discovered there was much more to him than being a simple farmer.

Jesse was a good man doing his best. Our marriage had worked out, but I had been the source of many of his problems. I needed to address them. I had rehearsed an apology in my mind many times. I needed to go back to Earth and get out of his life.

I couldn't look him in the eyes. The beautiful sheets covering my body were almost a work of art. "Jesse." I looked away from him. "I'm sorry. I never wanted these things to happen. I never meant for you to lose your farm and start running from the Bureau. You risked your life many times to save my sorry ass." I slapped my hand over my mouth, terribly aware I had sworn in front of him once again.

"Annalee," he said urgently. "It's okay if you swear. It doesn't offend me any longer."

I turned my head away, unable to keep the tears back.

"I made many mistakes. You and Porter could have been killed a dozen times over, and it's all my fault! I should go home. I don't belong here. I've never belonged and I never will."

"Ann," he crooned. "Don't say those words. They're not true. You don't have to be afraid. Let me tell you something."

He came around to the other side of the bed and gazed deeply into my eyes.

"I would do it all over again if I had to. Do you hear me? I would do everything as long as it meant you were going to be here with me at the end."

"But Jesse..." He cut me off gently, putting his fingers to my lips.

"No buts, Annalee," he said. "When I knew you were in a dungeon, and I couldn't do anything about it, I felt like my life was meaningless. I started thinking about the future. What would I do? Could I go on if I lost you?"

He stopped speaking for a minute. I was thinking about what he said, but I didn't want to say anything and interrupt his thoughts.

"I don't know what happened to me. I guess everything's changed." He put his hand to his head and stared at the floor. Eventually, he lifted his beautiful blue eyes to meet mine again.

"I love you, Annalee," he said taking my hand. "I love you. I don't think I can live without you anymore, so please don't talk about leaving again. I don't want you ever to leave me."

I couldn't lie there in bed any longer, and I had to get myself up. Even though it hurt, I managed to drag my poor battered body out of bed and sat on the edge, next to Jesse. He weaved his fingers into my hand.

"Do you think you might be able to stay on Yordbrook?" he said. "You still won't be able to have a phone, and you might not be a teacher here."

He was looking out the window, and it didn't seem like he wanted to stare at my face any longer.

"Jesse, look at me." I waited until he met my eyes. "I love you, too, Jesse. If you want me, I will never leave you, no matter what your planet does or doesn't have. It has you, and that's all that matters to me."

Like he said, everything had changed now.

CHAPTER 19

ANNALEE

We had chosen the inn near Jesse's home as a meeting place for one of the technology discussions.

It wasn't going well.

"What about the danger, Mr. Melnyk? We like our lives the way they are. No one has any desire to become a modern planet. I think the Queen is..."

"Mind your words," Porter growled.

The technophobe did a double-take at Porter's expression and rephrased his statement.

"The Queen is being imprudent in her attempt to bring technology back. I'm not the only one who thinks so."

There was a murmur of agreement from the crowd. Most of them knew Jesse as a branded misfit. Porter's reputation was that of a man who could get morelia or banned technology if you had something valuable to trade.

Now they were back in the community as the Queen's ambassadors. We were here to sell the idea of reintroducing technology into the daily lives of Yordbrook citizens. It was quite an intellectual leap. As an outsider, I could tell that some of the people wanted to support their regent in the new endeavor, but everyone was finding the concept difficult to understand.

As I watched them patiently and diplomatically respond to provocative questions and answer the serious queries, I felt a feeling of pride swell in my heart for my husband and friend. What they were doing for the Queen wasn't easy, but it would benefit an entire planet.

"I would love to message the men in the field when it's time for them to eat their dinner. Or remind my husband to come home from the inn without having to walk down here myself," said an older woman with a worn face. A few people chuckled. People were lost in their worlds, thinking about how they might use the devices that had been common in my other life.

A group of men started muttering to each other. I imagined one was the woman's husband, and he didn't want additional communication from his wife.

"What about electric lights? Ever since I was a child and heard about them in the Before Tales, I've always wanted to live in a house with lights I could turn on by flipping a switch."

"That brings up an important point," Jesse said, jumping into the conversation. "We would begin with simple things like electricity, devices for messaging, and wireless networks. But part of the royal edict requires the technology remain practically invisible."

"That's right," Porter added. "We'll start off slow. There are devices which stick on the inner forearm and are transparent when not in use. We can install concealed light switches. Our world can look the same on the outside, but be different underneath."

228

Jesse spoke up again. "The Queen plans to introduce laws that ensure the safe use of science for peaceful purposes." He looked around the room, meeting everyone in the eye. "We made a mistake long ago. It's time to forgive ourselves."

Many heads nodded, and the men closed the meeting for the night. Over the next few days, there would be other opportunities for people to express their opinions or ask questions. I was excited that this was the final stop on our rounds. We had been on the road for three months. I was tired of traveling.

Tonight we had the chance to use our bed in the guest house of the farm. I couldn't wait. I wanted to do something other than sleep; we hadn't had many chances to be alone since our near-execution.

The Queen had pressed Jesse and Porter into service right away. While I healed and rested at the palace, they went into the neighboring communities and tried to sell the Queen's philosophy to the people. Once I recovered, I joined them, and we took our show on the road. In each town, we stopped for three nights to talk to the locals, answer their questions, and calm their fears.

The other people in the Underground were doing the same thing. We were participating in a coordinated, planet-wide effort. Next month, the first shipment of forearm communicators was due to arrive in the capital. The vendors expected them to sell out on the first day.

I would get one, I supposed. But all I wanted was my phone with Kyle's picture on it. If I could see his little face again and send him a message his mother could read to him, I would feel less stupid about smuggling in the phone. In a small way, it would make everything worth it.

But I wasn't hopeful of ever getting my phone back. They had stored all the confiscated electronic devices at the palace. There was a lot of equipment - I guess people had used their technology but tried to keep it hidden. There were so many things there was a huge backlog returning them to their owners.

I would get my other possessions from Earth soon. I would even get my Internet-enabled glasses again. Soon I would be able to get online in the blink of an eye.

My mind drifted to other things that were impossible now, but would soon be commonplace on Yordbrook. As Jesse finished talking with the last person, he casually sauntered over to me.

"Well, woman? Shall I take you home to bed? You must be tired."

I nodded dutifully. The thought of him taking me to bed sent a pulse of energy through my body, and I didn't feel tired any longer. He lifted one eyebrow at me as if he could feel my body with his mind.

"We ought to leave right now then." He was suddenly in a rush.

"Where's Porter?"

"He's back in his room, writing a letter to the Queen. He can't wait to get back to her. These last three months have been a long time for all of us."

I knew he had sympathy for Porter and his troubles, but he didn't look sympathetic at all. He looked smug. He possessed a woman of his own, and I wanted him to take me.

He boosted me into the wagon. His touch made me gasp. As he climbed next to me, I felt electricity spark between us. We didn't speak, but I sensed I was about to be fucked to my core. With a terse command, the hundinlark moved forward away from the inn.

Jesse broke the silence first when he spoke my name. "Annalee." His voice sounded unnaturally deep in the quiet of the forest. "We will be alone in our house tonight."

"We will?" My voice sounded breathless, even to me.

He drew in a deep breath of his own and shifted in his seat. I imagined he was trying to restrain himself from taking me right here in the carriage.

"It has been a long time since our wedding night."

"It certainly has," I muttered to myself, then said aloud, "Indeed."

"I feel like I haven't been a proper husband to you." Well, if he was talking about fulfilling my sexual needs, then no, he definitely hadn't.

"I mean to rectify that tonight."

My heart started pounding. When we arrived at our house, he got down and helped me out.

"I'm going to take care of the hundinlark. Prepare yourself for me." Jesse leaned in to kiss me deeply before he headed toward the barns.

I scurried into the house and tried to get my dress off as quickly as possible.

JESSE

It was our four month anniversary today.

As I put the hundinlark in their stalls and started feeding them, I wondered if Annalee remembered. I unconsciously patted my pocket to make sure her present was still there. I hoped she liked it.

For a moment, I second-guessed myself. Maybe I should have gotten her a safer gift. I couldn't go wrong with a piece of jewelry. It had seemed perfect when I had seen it at the Bureau.

It was too late for a necklace, anyway. I would have to give her what I had and hope she liked it.

The hundinlark sensed my nervousness and snorted, stamping its foot. Even the animals could tell I was anxious. I was worrying too much.

My problem must be sexual frustration. I hadn't had Annalee since our wedding night. The past few months had been hectic. We barely had a moment alone together, and I felt like I was going insane. Sometimes I would catch a glimpse of cleavage or her ankle, and I would get hard. It was brutal, but the inns were full at this time of year, requiring us to share a room with Porter everywhere we went.

I had been looking forward to this night for a long time. I wondered if I would even last a few minutes. Maybe I could convince her to let off some steam first before we got to the main event. That would let me be a proper husband for her and make sure she came first. It would be embarrassing if I couldn't last for her, as if I were a teenager again.

I finished with the animals and hurried back to the house. It was silent and dark when I came through the front door. I carefully locked it behind me.

My heart sank. She was too tired to do anything tonight and had gone to bed early. I groaned. I felt like hitting the wall, but I didn't want my disappointment and frustration show. I dropped my head.

As my eyes looked down, the moonlight illuminated a piece of clothing on the floor. I bent down and saw that it was her dress. I picked it up. Why would she leave it here? Then I noticed her hood a couple of feet away and picked that up as well. Apparently her clothing was strewn all over the house. The next things I found was her stockings, followed by her shift.

My pulse started racing as I realized she had already shed her clothing, which meant when I found her...I continued to follow the trail of clothes, finding a corset at the bedroom door. I looked inside and saw a candle burning. Annalee lay on the bed, propped up by pillows…

She was completely naked.

I caught my breath, dropping the clothes I held onto the floor.

I had never seen anyone looking as beautiful as she did, gently illuminated by the candlelight. She looked nervous.

I don't know why the most beautiful woman on the planet would be nervous, but I felt compelled to speak.

"Annalee." My voice came out strangled, and I cleared my throat, making an attempt to be a gentleman. All I wanted to do at that moment was to fuck her, take her, and make her mine. "You look lovely."

"Thank you," she said demurely. "Now do you think you could come over here and fuck me?"

I froze for a moment. It was still surprising to hear her swear. She had read my mind, and we both wanted the same things. I tore off my clothes and was beside her in an instant.

"I don't think I can be slow."

"Who says I want anything slow? I asked you to fuck me before I go insane with lust, didn't I?"

"Yes." I covered her lips with mine. I broke away for a moment. "Porter didn't give you any morelia, did he?"

"I don't need morelia, Jesse. I've got you."

ANNALEE

Jesse tasted sweet, and his mouth was hot. I wanted to devour him. It had been a long time since we had shared a kiss that was more passionate than a peck on the cheek. I had avoided contact with him because I knew there was no chance to fulfill my desires.

Now that we had the opportunity to indulge, I felt lust overtake me. I had stripped off my clothing and left it in a sensual trail on the floor, leading to me. I had never done anything like that before; it was like a strip-tease frozen in time.

I trembled as I waited for him, nude on the bed. The shivering was a combination of nerves and desire. Now that he was here in my arms, I felt my body begin to react. I couldn't believe we had waited for such a long time.

We were tangled together, legs twisted, arms tightly clutching each other, tongues dancing. The ache between my legs was as bad as it had been with the morelia. When his hand slid around to my breast and began gently massaging it, I started to groan.

He pulled away suddenly. I missed his lips, but not for long. They closed around one of my tight buds.

"Oh God," I breathed. "Yes."

He sucked violently and I arched up toward him, needing him to take more of me. He let go and focused on my other nipple. He licked around it, then blew on the wet

236

skin, making me shiver. He kissed all the way around it, making me restless.

"Jesse." I pushed my breast toward him. He smiled and gave me what I needed. His scorching lips closed around the hardened nub, and I moaned, feeling wetness pooling between my legs.

I reached for him. His hard, smooth cock made me gasp.

"I need you inside me. Now."

His eyes fluttered closed, and his leg nudged between mine, spreading them. I felt him at my entrance. I spread wider, my whole body on fire. He pushed in, and I felt my heat surround him.

"Ann." My name came out of his lips sounding like a plea or a prayer. I wasn't sure which one. He gave a quick thrust and filled me completely.

We both lay together for a moment without moving, relishing in the sensation of joining again. When Jesse began to move inside of me, a small sound escaped my lips. He kissed me again, long and sweet, while he thrust in and out of my body. My orgasm built until I was right on the edge, my nipples brushing his hard chest as he moved. He was fucking me too slowly for what I needed right now.

"I need you to fuck me hard. Please," I begged. I was close. I needed him to push me over the edge.

He didn't say words but gave a hard, quick thrust that made me gasp.

"Yes. Like that." I pushed my hips toward him at the same time as he drove into me again.

Harder and faster, he pounded into me, and I felt him hitting the spot inside me that I had never noticed until we first made love. I was sure they heard my cries at the main house. I didn't care.

He bent his head and sucked my breast. That was enough to send me over the peak. I cried out and came, the climax shattering me and rocking my body with violent shudders. I held on tightly to Jesse. When I finally lay still, he plunged into me again, faster and faster until he froze and I felt him filling me with his seed.

I lay back, my bones feeling like water. I was so relaxed that I couldn't have moved if I tried.

"I love you, Annalee Beauchene," he whispered in my ear.

I remembered how I had thought my life was going to be. I guess life has a way of turning out differently than we expect.

Jesse pulled out, and I made a small sound of regret. He got out of bed. "I'll be back."

"I've heard that before."

"Really! Just a moment!" He returned almost immediately and jumped into bed. I snuggled up to him, melting into his body even though his skin was cold.

"I have a gift for you," he said. "It's our four month anniversary today."

"It is?" I didn't realize it myself. I was surprised he had remembered and gotten me something.

"It's not much of a present, but I thought you might like it."

He brought out a small thing. It was hidden in his hand until he put it in my palm.

"My phone! Where did you get it?" I had never been more thankful for solar-powered batteries. I turned it on and scanned my retina to unlock it. I flipped through screen after screen. Everything was still there; no one had tampered with anything.

"The Bureau had it. I was there one day when they were going through the confiscated items. For most devices, they can't identify the proper owners, and they're either scrapped or sold. I was lucky to find yours."

I turned it off and tapped it again to wake it up. The lock screen showed the picture of Kyle and me.

"You should thank him." I pointed to my little friend's picture.

"What? Why? I've never seen that child before."

239

"He's the reason everything's as good as it is right now. Even though we came through some bad shit to get here."

He ran a finger down my nose. "It's over, Ann."

"Yeah," I said. "It felt great to go back to the dungeon and get Jemima out. She never thought I would come back for her."

I smiled warmly at the thought. We had gone to visit her a few times. I would always be thankful for how she had helped me. But Jesse wasn't thinking about Jemima. He stared at the little boy on the screen.

"That's the kid whose picture you promised to keep with you, isn't it."

I nodded.

"Well, then, thanks, little man, for bringing this beautiful woman into my bed and my life," he whispered, kissing my neck.

"Beautiful?" I pushed him away for a minute, ignoring what his kisses did to me. "I remember you thought I was distinctly plain when we first met."

"I don't know why." His kisses moved lower onto my collarbone. "I was a fool."

I pushed him away. "Do you honestly think I'm beautiful now?" I felt skeptical. I took his head in my hands and made him look at me. "I know you think I'm sexy, but that's not the same thing."

He looked at me in consternation. I wondered if he could understand why this was important to me.

"Annalee, your spirit is infectious. It shines through your skin and makes everything around you radiant. Your eyes sparkle, your smile lights up a room, and your curves are perfect. Whoever thought you plain didn't know anything about you."

"Really?" I asked. I wasn't fishing for compliments, but I still couldn't believe his change of heart, no matter how much I knew he loved me.

"You have something that makes people sit up and take notice. You don't even know it, do you? That's part of the charm."

He returned to kissing and made his way down between my breasts.

"Thank you," I said, setting my phone down on the bedside table. I would have time to reacquaint myself with it later.

Right now, my husband was kissing me. He loved me and thought I was beautiful. I realized how far I had come since my days on Earth. I had followed my heart instead of my head. I knew I never wanted to go back to the old me because I wanted to be here forever.

CHAPTER 20

ANNALEE

I walked into the house and saw Mrs. Boyko sweeping up. As I watched, she kicked open a small vent near the floor and pushed against a knot in the wooden paneling on the wall. A soft humming noise sounded through the house as all the dirt she had swept got sucked away into the vent.

"If I had known technology would make my life this easy, I would have joined the Underground a long time ago." she said.

I grinned, shifting the little girl resting against my hip to my other side so I wouldn't have to put her down. She was getting heavy.

"And how is my little angel?" said Mrs. Boyko, jiggling Charlotte's foot until she smiled and pressed her face shyly into my shoulder.

"She's much better now, thanks to you." "She doesn't have a fever anymore. It's a relief."

"I didn't do much," she said. "Just applied some herbs, the same as my Granny used to give me. We don't need science for everything."

"You're right, of course." I kissed my daughter on the cheek. "In fact, that's why I came to see you.

"Oh?" She looked surprised and curious.

"I wondered if you could teach me what you know about herbs and plants. I'm interested in learning how to cure my children naturally."

"You only have one child." The woman looked at me accusingly.

"Damn. Jesse's going to be upset. I wasn't supposed to tell anyone yet."

"I would have guessed, dear. I won't say anything if you don't want me to."

I blushed. "Thank you. We'd like to tell people ourselves after I'm in my second trimester."

"Of course. Have you told your mother already?"

I stared down at the brilliantly clean floor while my daughter played with one of my braids. "I don't think I will." I stared off into the distance. "My mother's not too interested in my life these days."

Mrs. Boyko clucked a few times and patted me on the shoulder. I tried to think happy thoughts so I wouldn't look as hurt as I felt.

"I don't know her, but if what you say is true, she seems a foolish woman. She's missing out on a wonderful family and a special daughter."

That made me feel better. A smile broke out on my face.

"I suppose," I said. "I feel like Charlotte has a grandmother in you."

"Stop, Annalee! You'll make me start crying."

I gave her a hug, feeling a little close to tears myself.

"But what about your genetic grandchildren?"

"I try not to make that distinction. I don't talk about *real* or *fake* grandchildren. I have blood grandchildren and the grandchild of my heart. Charlotte is not better or worse than the others."

"Do you have any pictures of them?" I wanted to take my mind off how sweet Mrs. Boyko was before I lost control and broke down into sobs.

She pulled out a computer and touched her thumb on the screen, opening the lock.

I put on my 'Technology Consultant' hat for a moment. "It would be easier if you used a retinal scan, Mrs. Boyko. We can set it up tomorrow evening when Jesse and I come over for Sunday dinner."

"Whatever you say, dear." After some fiddling, beautiful pictures for me to admire appeared on her screen. "I will come by at naptime every day and we can teaching you herbalism. I'm happy to share my knowledge with you, Annalee."

It was like I had found the mother I never had before. And there was life after teaching. I would discover another passion and interest in plant life. I couldn't wait to start my new studies.

I strolled out of the main homestead and into the yard, headed toward the guest house. Unofficially it was my home, but we would always refer to the building as the guest house.

When I reached our steps, I heard a carriage approach behind me. I turned and shaded my eyes from the sun. I saw the profile of Marsaline, the Queen of Yordbrook, poking her head out the window of the carriage.

Charlotte was sleeping in my arms, taking a nap. I hurried into the house and laid her in the middle of our big bed. Jesse's cousin was cleaning the kitchen. I asked her to listen in case Charlotte woke up. The young woman often watched my daughter when I needed a babysitter. I didn't mind leaving my daughter while Marigold was there.

I ran to meet Marsaline emerging from her conveyance.

"Marsaline!" I spoke without thinking and covered my mouth in embarrassment. "I apologize. I mean, your Majesty. Why have you graced us with your presence?"

She looked around to see if anyone was near enough to overhear us. When she had determined to her satisfaction that no one was, she answered me truthfully.

"I want to see him, Annalee."

Marsaline and Porter had been separated for some time. She had been busy, not only changing the laws about science and technology, but also modifying the restrictions on who was eligible to marry royalty. Until they passed new legislation, Porter and Marsaline were pretending they barely knew each other.

"Come with me."

No one in the house had noticed the Queen's arrival. Her driver was rushing to put away the carriage. Without seeing the Queen or her transport, no one would know her whereabouts until she chose to reveal herself.

Porter had a retreat in the woods nearby. He kept himself busy running a technology import business and writing software. Once he had the opportunity, he found out he loved computers.

"How goes your work with the council?"

That was one of the problems with a monarchy combined with a representative democracy. The elected officials were resistant to any change, but Marsaline had royal blood. She was surprisingly effective in getting her way with things that were important to her.

"I believe we have reached an accord." She was barely paying attention to me, focusing on her search of the forest in front of us.

"It's finished? What about the other thing?"

"We can finally get married, if that's what you're implying. Marriage requires two people, however, and I need to find my fiance."

I checked off some boxes in my mental checklist. "What about Controller Kozel?" I wondered if she was still at large.

"We deported the *former* Controller, Annalee. You don't need to be afraid of her anymore."

I was surprised at how relieved I felt to hear those words. I had recurring nightmares she would find me and exact vengeance even though the Queen had removed her from the position. Now that I had confirmation of her departure, I felt myself relaxing.

In another minute, we were at Porter's quarters. It looked like a huntsman's lodge on the outside, but Porter redid the interior to his specifications. We saw him coming out the door.

His eyes were bright. "The computer said it was you, but I didn't believe it."

Jesse appeared behind him and my breath caught in my throat. I felt like he was only looking at me. He ran to me and gave me a kiss on the cheek. Part of me wanted to run away with him, but I couldn't stop my eyes from looking at the scene unfolding before us. I know I should have left. For some reason, I needed to see how the relationship between Porter and the Queen played out.

"The Queen wants to see you." She pulled back her hood, revealing light brown hair in a simple braid. It was nothing like the elaborate hairstyle she wore at the palace.

Porter was mesmerized by the sight of her bare head. He reached out his hand to gently smooth her hair away from her forehead. They spoke as if we weren't there.

"Enough to leave when the parliament remains in session?"

"I did it, Porter. It's finished. We can get married now."

Porter held her face in his hands and kissed her passionately. Jesse tugged on my hand, pulling me away.

"Porter's going to be the Queen's consort," Jesse said with a laugh.

"It's unbelievable," I said. "Too bad he can't be the king. He'll remind her of the days when she was a commoner and keep her relaxed."

"And she'll help him upgrade his style," Jesse added. "They're perfect for each other."

"Just like us," I said, swinging his hand as we walked through the forest.

He stopped and gently tugged my hand, pulling me into his arms. I happily wrapped my hands around his neck.

"I love you, Annalee. But are you happy here? I worry that our lives are too dull, and I know you miss life on Earth." Concern filled Jesse's eyes as he waited for my answer.

"For the last time, I didn't enjoy my modern life. I worked too hard. I was lonely. I have more time to relax here, and I've got you..." I cupped his cheek with my hand. "And Charlotte. Mrs. Boyko is more of a mother to me than mine has ever been. And everyone. I love my life and my new job."

"I don't know. Is there anything else you want?" His eyes twinkled.

I locked my eyes on his.

"Let me think." I tapped my head, pretending to consider it. "How about an hour alone with you and we'll call it even?"

"Mrs. Boyko has been asking me why we don't let her watch the little one. It seems like a good time to call in the favor."

My body hummed with anticipation at the thought of spending time alone with my husband.

"Charlotte is napping," I said.

"Come on, Annalee. I know what we can do with our free time."

"Whatever you desire, husband," I said. My face flushed, and I dropped my eyes as if I were a demure Yordbrook wife.

"I know a place where we can go to be alone."

"Alone?" I said. "I'm never alone with you, Jesse."

It was the truth. I wouldn't want it any other way.

If you enjoyed this book, please review it on Amazon. Your review helps me succeed as an author.

To stay up-to-date on my latest releases, sign up for my newsletter at:

http://lisalace.com/newsletter/

OTHER BOOKS BY LISA LACE

WATER WORLD WARRIOR: A TerraMates Novel

Why would I want to be married to an alien?

I should not have applied to TerraMates! The idea was crazy. I'm a young woman, in the prime of my life.

But I was desperate.

When I landed on another world, his appearance intrigued me. He dripped sexuality and moved like an animal. We have three days together before he sets sail without me. Am I going to escape or submit to my desires?

TAKEN: A TerraMates Novel

What happens when TerraMates runs out of applicants?

There's never a shortage of wealthy alien bachelors looking for the thrill of mating with a human. They want our women.

But despite the promise of riches, sometimes the pool of available brides runs dry.

How does TerraMates find more girls, and where do they go? When Lyzette gets taken off the street, she finds out.

WATER WORLD CONFIDENTIAL: A TERRAMATES NOVEL

He needed a wife. I wanted an alien lover.

The first time I saw Jori, I hated everything about him. He didn't care about anything except himself. On the other hand, his body was spectacular, and his muscles were firm. I couldn't stop thinking about him.

When TerraMates gave me the chance to marry Jori, I took it. I knew I needed the money. What I didn't know was that Jori's exterior was a facade, and he had kept secrets from everyone his entire life.

ALPHA'S ENSLAVED BRIDE: A TERRAMATES NOVEL

Knowing the future isn't a blessing. It's a curse. Especially when you've seen your death.

I'm going to die in the arms of someone I have never seen before. He's a person I will love, but I don't know anything about him.

When TerraMates matched me with Airik, I couldn't believe it. This sexy alien could see the future, just like me. I wasn't alone anymore. I quickly found out he knows nothing about Earth or humans. I married him, but will I be safe with him?

I didn't foresee I would want to feel his hands on my body.

I've never been able to change the future before. For us to survive, I need to.

Auctioned to the Alpha: A TerraMates Novel

The innovative TerraMates business has been a runaway success. Who wouldn't want to marry an alien?

Seeking to expand, TerraMates has opened new locations with different business models.

Eden is looking for a fresh start and is one of the first mail-order brides from New York City. As soon as she signs the paperwork and collects her credits, she blacks out.

When Eden wakes up, she's been married to an alien bounty hunter. She's ready for a new beginning, but all she knows about her alien husband is that he's handsome and dangerous. Eden never dreamed she'd be chasing criminals through space!

Captured by the Alien King

When I saw my chance to get off Earth, I took it. I knew I needed to escape.

I didn't know I'd be claimed by an alien monarch in the middle of his mating season! Now we're on the run together, facing terrorists and natural disasters.

I'm still trying to figure out my feelings for this sexy guy. He is totally into me, but he has some unique ideas about alien romance…